TO MADDEN A MARQUESS

Lords of London, Book 2

TAMARA GILL

COPYRIGHT

To Madden a Marquess
Lords of London, Book 2
Copyright © 2018 by Tamara Gill
Cover Art by Wicked Smart Designs
Editor Authors Designs
All rights reserved.

ISBN-13: 978-0-6484133-1-8
ISBN-10: 0-6484133-1-4

DEDICATION

For all the fabulous readers in the Hellions Reader Group. Thank you for being such a wonderful group of friends.

CHAPTER 1

Cecilia Smith stood on Curzon Street and tried to hail a Hackney cab. The streets were busy with coal carts, people walking along the cobbled footpath and gentlemen with their ladies out for an afternoon stroll. Cecilia pulled her spencer closed as a light breeze chilled the air, and waved to another Hackney that too, trotted past without a backward glance.

What was going on? Did they not see her? The thought was probably closer to the truth than she liked to admit. Here in Mayfair, in the drab, working-class gown that she was wearing, it was any wonder no one bothered to stop to pick her up. The working populace that was her sphere wasn't well-to-do enough for this locale, and it had not passed her notice that a lot of those out and about had thrown her curious, if not annoyed glances her way that she'd dared enter their esteemed realm.

From the corner of her eye, a flash of black arrested her attention. Turning to look, she observed as a gentleman stumbled toward a street lamp, leaning up against it as if it were the only thing keeping him upright.

He was a tall gentleman, his clothing was cut to perfection, and fit his tall, muscular frame well, but his eyes that she could see even from across the road were blood-shot with dark rings beneath them.

Was he ill, suffering apoplexy or merely drunk?

A hackney cab barrelled down the road and showed no signs of slowing. Cecilia turned her attention back to the gentleman and horrifyingly watched as he started across the busy thoroughfare.

Without a moment's hesitation she started toward him, and looking toward the hackney cab wasn't sure if even she would make it out of its way before it was too late. What an absurd, stupid man for putting himself and now her also in danger. Did these Mayfair dandies have no sense?

He stumbled just as she made his side, and heaving him with all of her might thumped him hard in the chest, sending him to fly backward and toward the safety of the side of the road. Unfortunately, he reached out at that very moment and brought her down with him. The man's head made a loud crack as it hit the cobbled pavement.

The hackney cab rattled past without so much as a by-your-leave and Cecilia scrambled to her feet and stood next to the man, peering down at him. The scent of spirits wafted from him, almost as if he'd bathed in the stuff and his uncertain footing and stupid attempt to cross the road without care was all too clear. Nevertheless, she couldn't just leave him there, even if she really wanted to. How lovely it would be to be able to prance about town at midday, drunk and without a care, as this fellow seemed to do. He must be one of those rich nobs that waltzed at balls and believed everything that was said or written about them was true.

If only they knew that her class laughed and mocked them at every turn. If it weren't for her kind, London would screech to a halt, no matter what the upper ten-thousand thought. They might make the laws, employ many, but it was her lot in life that kept the city running, and the country counties too when she thought about it.

He moaned, and she kneeled beside him, tapping his cheek lightly. His clothing smelt of stale wine, his breath reeked of spirits and a hard night, not to mention there was a slight odor of sweat that permeated the air. When he didn't respond to another gentle prod, she gave him a good whack. His eyes opened, his dark blue orbs wide in shock before narrowing in annoyance. This close to him, Cecilia noticed his sharp cheekbones, strong jaw and his too perfectly shaped nose was probably prettier than her own.

"What do you think you're about hitting me like that? Have care, miss, miss, miss."

She stood and held out her hand. He gazed at it in confusion before she sighed and leaning down again, took his hand in hers. "Stand, before you're nearly run over again by another carriage. And do be quick about it. I'm late for my meeting already."

He moaned as he allowed her to help him up. Cecilia led him onto the footpath and ensured he was well off the road before she let go of his hand. "Is your home nearby? Can I escort you there to ensure your arrival is to a satisfying end, unlike the one you almost had on the road just now?"

He frowned, rubbing his forehead. "I was on the road?"

"Yes, you were. Just how foxed are you sir?"

"I'm not a sir," He replied with an arrogant tilt of his head.

Cecilia took a calming breath to prevent herself from pushing the imbecile back onto the road. Really. Wasn't a sir? "Pray tell me, what are you then? I'm sure it's important that I must know to correct my silly ways?"

"Are you being sarcastic?" A small quirk turned his lips. Cecilia found her attention riveted on the spot and she vexed herself that she would be so pathetic as to look at his mouth at such a time.

"You are a smart one, sir."

"I would have you know, I'm the Marquess of Aaron, Hunter to my friends. Hunt for those of even closer acquaintance."

"Well, aren't we vulgar." Cecilia stepped away from him, dusting down her gown after their collision. "If you're safe and well enough to manage to get yourself home before you're struck by another vehicle I shall leave you now." Cecilia turned and started down the pavement. She left the marquess standing behind her, his agape mouth the last memory she'd have of him. She smiled a little, imagining he'd not been talked to so abruptly before. Not that he didn't deserve to be brought down a level or two.

"Wait!" he demanded, his footsteps hastened as he came up beside her. "You didn't tell me your name."

Since his lordship was so particular about titles, Cecilia decided to play a little trick on him. "I am the Duke of Ormond's daughter. Heir to a massive fortune and looking for a husband."

He started. "Really?"

"No. Not really. I'm Miss Cecilia Smith. My father owns and runs J Smith & Sons, Lawyers and I reside in Cheapside if you must know. I am also late for a charity meeting. So if you do not mind, I shall leave you to your stupor and go."

She moved on and ignored the light chuckle she heard behind her. He didn't follow, but she felt the heat of his gaze on her back. It was a pleasant feeling knowing he was watching her, not that she would ever see him again. Their social spheres were eons apart and he would only look to her Society for mistresses. Never marriage, unless it was absolutely necessary due to financial woes or some other such reason.

And as much as she hated to admit it, Cecilia had heard of the Marquess of Aaron and the wild and naughty antics the rich toff was known for around London. If what they wrote in the papers about him was accurate, he was a man who lived life fast and hard and left a bevy of young women pining for him to marry them. It was rumored that if he asked for a dance, they were instantly in love with him.

Cecilia rolled her eyes, not impressed by her first encounter with the gentleman. Waving again to a Hackney coming toward her, she sighed in relief when it pulled up, and she was able to travel the few blocks to her destination. The carriage rocked to a halt on the corner of Fleet Street and St Bride's Avenue. Cecilia stepped down from the carriage, paid the driver before turning her attention to the meeting at Old Bell Tavern where she wanted to press her idea for another orphanage and school on Pilgrim Street in Ludgate where a large, unoccupied building currently sat. Her father had promised her the funds, and now all she had to do was get the women at her meeting to agree and then all her plans would come to fruition. It was the right thing to do, and she was sure she wouldn't have any trouble getting them to agree.

If she managed to be instrumental in making just one of the orphaned children of London have a good stable job that enabled them to live a full and happy life, then her work at the charity was worth it. It was the best day in the world when children who'd arrived, sick and poor left and became house and ladies' maids, cooks even, if their inclination leaned them in that direction. The boys becoming footmen, stable hands and those who were mathematically inclined, stewards even. If one wanted to change, one had to work toward the goal and not believe everything would just fall in your lap.

With invigorated stride, Cecilia pushed open the doors at the Bell Tavern and headed for the private parlor where they always had their meetings. Life was excellent, and she was about to make it even better, especially for those who lived on the streets that had no life at all. Not yet at least.

CHAPTER 2

Hunter watched the hellcat disappear down the street. She produced a lovely view for him from behind, the cut of her gown, no matter how plain and dull, didn't take from the small waist, plentiful bosom and delectable bottom that swayed a little with each step. Miss Smith was a tall woman, and it brought forth the image of how lovely and long her legs would be, how far about his waist they would go during certain physical exercise…

He blinked as a bout of dizziness assailed him, and he clasped the oil lamp on the footpath to steady his stance. Hell, he needed a drink. His mouth was as dry as the Egyptian desert. A matron walked by and looked down her nose in distaste. Bowing, Hunter went to tip his hat, and his hand met with thin air.

What the devil happened to his hat! He'd left Whites late and tumbling into a carriage, remembered meeting a good friend for some late night gambling near St James Park. He'd meant to end the night at his mistress's boudoir, but apparently, he'd not made it there at all. Hunter frowned, rubbing a hand over his jaw. In truth, he had no idea what the night had entailed or how much he'd lost at the tables.

Walking on, he looked back to where Miss Cecilia Smith had disappeared. She was long gone, and a pang of regret pierced him that he wouldn't see her again. Not many women would openly show their distaste for his current appearance including the fact he was still as foxed as he was last evening.

She had a certain spunk about her that he couldn't help but admire. He supposed finding a woman who was so blunt, crass almost was more prominent in the middle class, since so many ladies had to work alongside their husbands and fathers. And here in London, there were many such women.

Hunter made the curb and hailed down a Hackney Cab. No more walking, his stomach churned, and it was probably best that he didn't cast up his accounts all over the street. The cab pulled up and flicking the driver a coin, Hunter settled onto the squabs. He would go home, bathe and retire to bed. Tonight Lord Stone was hosting a men's only evening that included exotic dancers from…. Hunter grimaced, not able to remember, but knowing they would be as beautiful as they were favourable with their affections.

He smiled and shut his eyes, resting for a moment. What a wonderful, decadent, indulging life he led. May his life never end.

CECILIA STOOD before the members of the London Relief Society and glowered. "What do you mean we cannot open a new orphanage and school on Pilgrim Street? The building is there, vacant and derelict. We simply need to find out who owns it and then purchase the damn place."

"Ladies, please. Allow Miss Smith to explain before we all dismiss this latest idea," the Duchess of Athelby said, staring down the few women who'd argued with Cecilia over the last ten minutes. "Cecilia deserves to have her say."

The duchess, a woman of high importance in the *ton*, was a welcome addition to their members, and she'd joined not long after she'd married the duke. Over the past year, they had become good friends. The duchess was a woman genuinely willing to help those less fortunate.

Her friend, Katherine Martin whose father was a well-known and respected builder in London raised her hand, capturing everyone's attention. "All Miss Smith is trying to say is that we should not give up so easily. Those of us here from working-class families know when things get tough we simply pull up our sleeves and get the work done. There is no difference here. We can and will do this. We must."

Cecilia smiled at her friend who always supported her. They had grown up together, had lived next door to each other in Cheapside for as long as Cecilia could remember.

"The building is too broken down to house children, and I still think we should direct funds to the schools we already have," Miss Tapscott said, her prude little mouth mottling up and reminding Cecilia of the back end of a dog.

Cecilia fought not to roll her eyes. "Miss Tapscott, we cannot simply turn a blind eye to the need that is prevalent in Ludgate, why, a lot of London's boroughs in fact. I agree the building does need work, but we have family, parents even who own and run varied trades in London and beyond. If any women are suitable to get this building transformed into a school and home for those less fortunate, to turn around their lives and give them some chance, then it is us."

"She's right, and Miss Tapscott," Katherine said, standing, "your father owns a mill. Surely you could persuade him to donate some lumber to rebuild the parts of the building that are in need of repair."

"I'm sure I could persuade my father to help with the supply of wood. He has many men working beneath him you know. He's quite successful even if he doesn't get up to London much," Miss Tapscott said, giving a pointed glance at Cecilia.

"Very good and I'll instruct my father to find out who owns the building and we'll commence with the purchase of it. I'm sure if we find the owner, who obviously does not use or wish to use the building of concern, we'll be able to persuade them to sell." Cecilia slipped her notes into her little leather carry bag, announcing the end of the meeting. "We'll regather here next week at the same time. Our duties are to find out what help and assistance our families and friends can be toward this new school and home for underprivileged children. Are we all in agreement?"

The seven ladies present concurred, and within a few minutes, Cecilia and Katherine started toward the tavern's door.

"Good meeting today and I'm so pleased we were able to talk the ladies around to see the benefits of having the new school built. The number of children who require our help are growing daily, and in Ludgate, there isn't a facility like ours, and it's sorely needed."

"I agree," Cecilia said, opening the door for her friend before going to the curb and hailing a hackney. "Father will help me track down the people who own the building and then we'll be able to move forward with our plans." A hackney arrived after much waving was had.

Katherine climbed up and slammed closed the carriage door. "We're to attend the Opera tonight. I wonder if Mr. Elton will be present."

"I'm sure he will be, and you'll be swooning all over him again. Not that you should. He's a little old for you."

"He is only thirty, Cecilia." Katherine grinned and looked out the window. "But I do like him. What a shame he's courting Miss Tapscott."

"Emily has nothing on you." Cecilia sighed thinking about her own run in this afternoon with the obnoxious Marquess of Aaron. "Did I tell you who I had the unfortunate event of saving today?" A little shiver ran over her skin at the thought of him. Of how close he'd been to being hit by the hackney. What a drunk fool he was and what a shame that was the case. For should the marquess be appropriately attired, not dishevelled from the night before and the revelry he so obviously took part in, he'd be very handsome indeed.

Oh, who was she fooling? He was handsome in any way he was presented.

Katherine turned her full attention toward Cecilia. "Who? You never mentioned running into anyone before the meeting."

"I was late if you remember, and the reason for that was the very handsome, very rakish Marquess of Aaron. I was walking down Fleet Street when I noticed the man stumbling along, and then the fool thought to walk out in the middle of the road and try and be hit by a cab. What else was I to do but save the prig."

Her friend's eyes widened. "And did you?"

"Did I what?" Cecilia asked, frowning.

"Save him!"

She laughed. "Oh yes, I got him off the road without any harm done to his absurdly beautiful bone structure.

But I really ought to have let him be hit. No man should ever be that perfect."

Katherine laughed. "You bantered with a marquess. Oh, what a story to tell your grandchildren one day. He's famous about London. Everyone wants to be his friend and be part of his set. He is known to be vastly naughty and flirts with even the old matrons in the *ton*. And you saved his life. He owes you."

"He doesn't owe me anything. In all honesty, I was glad I was there to help him for he was as foxed as they come."

"In the middle of the day, his lordship was drunk?" Katherine sighed, sitting back in the squabs. "This shouldn't surprise me as I've heard other rumors about his lordship."

"What rumors are they?" Cecilia tore her gaze away from the streets outside their carriage that slowly started to meander their way into their neighbourhood, a much less savoury one than the one the marquess would hail from.

"That he's always inebriated. That there hasn't been an outing he's attended this year where he hasn't been foxed or in such a state by the time he leaves. It really is a great shame that he isn't able to attend balls and parties without being so drunk. His lordship might find that he enjoys himself more if he wasn't in such a state, but so far not many have seen him otherwise. I suppose his wayward life could be blamed on his parents."

Cecilia didn't like the idea of the Marquess having such demons. Indeed today when she'd saved him it had been in the middle of the afternoon. Most people of his set were sleeping the day away, gaining their strength for the next night's entertainments. But his lordship had not been. He'd still been returning home from who knows where. The smell of him certainly wasn't pleasant as one would expect a nob to be. Was what Katherine saying true? How terrible if it was so.

"His parents? What do you mean?" Cecilia asked.

Katherine met her gaze. "His parents before they passed away were famous for their public arguments, their lively love-hate relationship." She shrugged. "Although I've not heard Lord Aaron has acted in such a way in public with a woman, he's certainly as wild as his sire was behind doors."

"How do you know all this about the marquess? I've never heard you mention his name before today."

"I read the paper, but also, my ladies' maid has a sister who works for the marquess, just as a scullery maid. Even so, the stories that she's been told about his lordship, the parties that take place at his townhouse, the company he keeps and what they get up to is beyond anything we've ever imagined. There will be stories told about his lordship for years to come I'm sure, even after his death."

Which would be sooner rather than later if he kept up such antics. Walking out in front of carriages indeed. Stupid, handsome fool.

LATE THAT AFTERNOON, Hunter lay back in his bath and groaned when his servant knocked on his bathroom door.

"My lord, your steward would like a word with you downstairs in the library when you're ready. He's willing to wait."

"Tell him to come up here and speak. I'll not have my bathing rushed." He'd only just got into the damn tub for crying out loud, and with any luck, the pounding headache he currently suffered with would abate a little in the warm, soothing water that smelt of lavender.

Hunter rested his head back on the tub and looked up at his ornate ceiling that had cherubs floating about in clouds. Really, the image was absurd, but a reoccurring effect upon the ceilings throughout his home.

The thought of another who had a rounded ass just like the cherubs above him floated into his mind. Miss Cecilia Smith. A very plain name for a woman who was completely the opposite of that. She was extremely attractive for a woman of the middle class, untitled, located in a different part of London and their social circles couldn't be more different. But she was extraordinarily beautiful.

Her ethereal golden locks had sat tied on the top of her head, little wisps floating about her face with the most striking, intelligent blue eyes he'd ever beheld. She'd saved his life, and for the life of him, he couldn't remember if he'd thanked her.

And nor would he get the chance now, since it was unlikely he'd ever see her again. A shame for he'd love to get to know her better. He was in need of setting up a new mistress, his current one was too needy, had become a whiny little thing who was no longer fun. Maybe a woman of Miss Smith's class would accept such a proposition from him. He dismissed the idea as soon as he had it, she had a father who was in law, would have family and friends who expected her to marry well, she would not be looking to be his lover, no matter how rich he'd make her.

He started when a loud knock sounded on his bathroom door. "Come in," he said, sighing as his thoughts and ideas for the delectable Miss Smith vanished from his mind.

"My lord, apologies for interrupting you, but I have some urgent business matters which must be discussed."

"And they are?" he asked, flicking a glance at his man of business Mr. Marsh. His steward was a tall gentleman, but too thin by far, looked as if a good meal would kill him. His hair was washed and kept pulled back from his face, that had an overly broad forehead. He was smart man and hence why he was working for Hunter. Probably a good thing that his forehead was so broad, if only to hold in his massive mind.

"The property on Pilgrim Street that is empty has had an offer of purchase against it." He ruffled through his papers. "Ah, the charity by the name of London Relief Society wish to meet and negotiate a price."

Hunter sat up in the bath. "That property is marked for development for a gentleman's club for the middle class as it were. Building for it was to commence next year. Why is anyone offering on it? The property was taken off the market months ago." He had the idea for a gentleman's club for the middle class, to give those who were bankers, lawyers or barristers a place to go and enjoy good wine, food and intelligent company. It had been one of his best ideas, and it was now in the final stages of planning and design.

"I believe, my lord that they wish to open up a school for the children who need it, an orphanage of some kind."

The location made sense, as in that part of town there were hundreds of kids running about, their parents either working or unfortunately dead and unable to keep track of them. In this part of London, the seedier side of the city was kept at bay, not spoken about and relatively ignored. Hunter had wanted to revamp the area a little, offer it a little luxury to those who lived and worked there. Putting an orphanage and school did not suit that plan at all.

"How much did they bid for the building in its current state?" Hunter asked, having not thought he'd ever have anyone interested in the site.

"Two hundred and fifty pounds, my lord."

An excellent sum, but still no gentleman's club. "And when does this charity wish to meet?"

His steward ruffled through his papers once again. "The meeting is set for tomorrow at four in my offices on Regent Street. The charity will attend and make their formal offer."

What was he doing tomorrow evening.... Ah, there was a card game at Whites he'd wanted to attend. Many a gentleman would be present who didn't play as well as they ought, and Hunter often left with a much more massive purse than the one he arrived with.

"Do we know who will be in attendance from this charity?" Hunter asked, his voice bored even to his own ears.

Again Mr. Marsh ruffled through his paperwork. "A Mr. John Smith and his daughter, Miss Cecilia Smith. Mr. Smith is the owner and barrister from J Smith and Sons."

Hunter sat up in the tub. *Miss Cecilia Smith*. Could it be the very one who'd saved and chastised him not hours ago? "I think I shall attend and hear what they have to offer. Although I have no intentions of selling, I have other business on Regent street and will be in the area. It is only right that I attend and notify this charity of my plans for the site."

"Very good, my lord. I will see you at four tomorrow," Mr. Marsh said, bowing and leaving him in peace.

Hunter shut his eyes, revelling in the warm, fragrant water. Tomorrow he would purchase a new phaeton carriage. Baron Abram had started to race them from London to his estate in Kent and Hunter wanted to take part. Now he would be able to and enjoy himself at the gambling parties that were hosted after such sport.

A capital idea if ever he had one.

CHAPTER 3

C ecilia Smith shut her mouth with a snap when the Marquess of Aaron sat down across from her in Mr. Marsh's office on Regent Street. Her breath hitched, and she swallowed the nerves that took flight in her belly. This could not be happening. Only days before their paths had crossed and now, again, here he was, staring at her with amusement that made her hackles rise, and her cheeks to heat.

To be sure nothing was out of place, Cecilia checked her attire and satisfied all was well, met his gaze. He didn't need to know she'd eaten a pastry prior to coming here, and it would have been just her luck that the crumbs were sitting upon her bottle green day dress.

The Marquess's steward started to discuss the plans for the building, and it was enough to bring Cecilia out of her musings on his lordship and concentrate at the job at hand.

"A gentleman's club! That is preposterous," she said, raising her chin. "The location is not Mayfair or Knightsbridge, it is Ludgate. We do not want your gentleman's clubs here. What is needed is more homes for those who are less fortunate than yourself."

Mr. Marsh's mouth pinched, and Cecilia smiled at him. She would not play this high and mighty lord's game. He would not make the London Relief Society start from scratch and find some other place to purchase. As the building stood, two-hundred and fifty pounds was probably more than they ought to offer, but it was paramount in their plans for the future, the children's future in this area and so they had offered a little more to make the deal tempting to the vendor. In this case, though, she had not thought the vendor would've been the marquess and a money hungry vulture one at that.

"The property, even in its current condition is valued more than what you've offered. But as I stated before, my client will be remodelling the building for a gentleman's club, not an orphanage."

Cecilia placed her hand on her father's arm when he went to speak, and instead caught the Marquess's eye. "Maybe his lordship, considering the fact that I saved his life only days ago, will rethink his plans with the building. Had I not stopped your foxed self from walking out in front of that hackney, you wouldn't even be here today to accept or reject our offer of purchase. Nor would you be able to make it a gentleman's club like you're so set to do."

He leaned back in his chair, smirking and Cecilia's stomach fluttered at his absurdly appealing visage. "Touché, Miss Smith, but I still will not sell you the building. I thought I would do right by your charity and meet with you, explain my plans, not negotiate another option."

Anger and disappointment surged through her veins. "Children are relying on us, children who'll never have a roof over their heads unless I supply that cover. Your belittling of their circumstances by wanting to make a frivolous, and boring gentleman's club, promoting affluent lifestyles that help no one, makes you look like an ass."

The steward gasped, and her father clasped her hand, shaking his head. "Cecilia, apologize to his lordship at once."

She ignored them all. "And while we're at it, let me remind you your building may be the most suitable, but it is not the only one available in that area. We can look elsewhere if need be, you may want to remember that." Even though it was suited best of all they'd viewed and would be the cheapest option available to them at this stage. But he didn't need to know that if he was playing hard for a higher offer.

The marquess leaned back in his chair and folded his arms across his chest. The action made his arms seem a lot larger than what she remembered them from the day before. In fact, today his lordship looked practically normal. Certainly he wasn't foxed, or sleep deprived as he had been. If anything, he had an air of intelligence that she hadn't thought he possessed.

"Had you offered twelve months past, I might have thought on the offer, but since then I have put in place plans for the remodelling and structuring of the building's usage. So now, unfortunately, Miss Smith you are out of luck."

"So it would seem," she said, standing and putting her notepad back in the leather case she carried to all her business dealings. "Come, father, this meeting is finished."

The marquess stood and held out his hand to her. Cecilia looked at it for a moment debating whether she really wanted to shake this man's hand or for that matter touch him at all. The last time she had, it left her feeling a little lost and not herself. It wasn't to be borne.

With a sigh she shook it, tightening her hand to the

point that he narrowed his eyes. Good, she wanted him to know she was no pathetic, whimpering miss that he could pull the wool over. She was an educated, worldly woman who could read this marquess like a book. He may be laughing at her now, thinking her a silly fool for trying to do business with a lord, but she would show him. Their dealings would not end here. And he would not win this war. Not today, or ever.

He arched a brow, a slightly sardonic smile slanting his lips. "What a strong handshake you have, Miss Smith. Almost masculine in fact."

She laughed, pulling him closer to her so that only they could be heard. "I will not play your game, nor will I allow you to build your gentleman's club. I think you should take some time and think over our final offer. I do not wish to, my lord, but the class I hail from is the very one you're trying to market to, and my father is well known. Your club will need members, yes? If you do not sell to me, I shall ensure no one of my set ever sets foot in your building."

He grinned, holding her tight and not letting her remove her hand from his grasp. "How very delightful you are, Miss Smith. Do tell me what else you have planned for my future. I am quite enraptured."

Cecilia wrenched her hand free. "Nothing more, my lord. I think what I stated is enough."

Taking a fortifying breath, she helped her father to stand as sitting for long periods tended to make him seize up a little. Walking outside, they were soon in the family carriage, heading back to the offices. Cecilia tugged her gloves off, slapping them against her skirts. "That man is the most vexing, arrogant, too high in the instep man I've ever met in my life. Not to mention one of the dumbest. A gentleman's club, for men like you, papa. How absurd."

"You were extremely blunt with the marquess. He could make your life, even in the small Society we grace hard for you to make a good match in marriage. You should watch how you speak to people, my dear. It is not becoming of you."

"Pfft. I don't care a fig if it's not becoming of me, he is a fool."

Her father frowned and studied her for a moment. "What did you mean when you said you saved his life two days past. Have you met the marquess before?"

Cecilia nodded and looked out the carriage window, the streets busy with shoppers and people out for strolls or calls. Not her though, at three and twenty she was a fortified spinster and solidly on the shelf just as she wished it to be. With her friends and her charity, she was never lonely or sad about her circumstances. If anything it enabled her to spend more time with the unfortunates of the world. And she'd much rather be with them, than tending to a husband, locked up at home day in and day out with nothing else to do but sew and host parties.

"I was running late for a meeting at the London Relief Society, and I spotted this man wandering, stumbling really onto the street. No one seemed to be taking any notice of the danger he was in, and I intervened. Stopped him from being hit by a passing carriage. I should've let him be flattened. I would've got my building then for two-hundred and fifty pounds. His estate would've sold it off right smart, just to be rid of it."

Her father scowled. "Cecilia you should not speak so vulgar. You're better than that. I know you have a good heart, and there will be other buildings. His loss and stubbornness will be your gain, mark my words."

The carriage pulled up in front of J Smith and Sons,

her father's offices. Cecilia glanced at the building's glass doors with her father's name which included 'and sons' on it. Not that she had any brothers, a point he never brought up, but the disappointment he felt was sometimes palpable in their home. If only women could be lawyers, bankers and stewards, and then 'and sons' could be replaced with the wording 'and daughter'. But it was not to be. Her father had chosen who would take over the firm after his death, and it was not her.

"Did you wish to come inside and see Mr. White? I know he'd like to see you again."

The man her father intended for her was Mr. Justin White, a pompous lawyer who had trained under her father and now helped run the firm. Cecilia couldn't stand the man, he was demanding and had not an ounce of empathy in his body, certainly not for her or her charities. As much as her father wished it, she would never marry the man. Even if he did end up inheriting her father's company.

If she ever married, and that was a very big if, she wanted a man who cared for those who were born less fortunate. Give time and money to her causes and try and make some change to these people's circumstances. A husband who would not expect her to be a wife, cossetted at home, seen but never heard. And certainly not a husband who did nothing but idle his life away in folly and meaningless pursuits. Like a certain marquess she could think of.

"I'll excuse myself this time, thank you, father. After today, I wish to return home in any case and have a long, hot bath. I need to wash off the autocratic, obstinate stench of Lord Aaron."

Her father chuckled and left her alone in the carriage. The remainder of the trip she stared sightlessly outside thinking about the marquess. How dare he deny her with little thought for the fortunes of others. Was he so unfeeling to so easily ignore what was needed for her charity, the children and families relying on them?

She wrung her gloves in her hands. No matter what she said to the gentleman's steward or her father for that matter, the building was really their only option. At this time there wasn't anything else on the market, and their limited refurbishment budget only went so far. The building next door to their preferred, although for sale, needed a lot more work, so unless they could get more funding, which was highly doubtful, his lordship's property was their only alternative. They simply must gain it in some way. If only she had kept check of her temper and not concluded the meeting prematurely. Sometimes her irritation really did get in the way of progress.

There simply must be a way to change his mind. Maybe she could ask him again, bring some unfortunate children with her so he could see why his building was so important to them. Make him see the struggles going on outside of his precious Mayfair.

Cecilia pursed her lips as an idea so delicious popped into her head. Oh yes, the marquess should she pull off this idea would sell to her, and quickly, especially with what she had in store for him. She called out to the driver, directing him to their Spitalfields orphanage and school. She needed a little help from her friends there. Poor Lord Aaron would be banging down her door to sell, and more than likely with her friends help, before the week's end.

HUNTER STROLLED down St James's Street, his cane a regular crescendo against the cobbled footpath as he headed for Whites. After his meeting with Miss Smith the previous week, he'd found he had no stomach to attend his allotted entertainments planned and had missed two balls and a picnic in Richmond Park. Most odd and unlike him. The vexing chit had annoyed him greatly, and not a little of what she said pricked his conscience. Never did he flaunt his wealth, his ability to spend whatever he wished, whenever he wished without a care to anyone else. Did he?

Surely he did not. It was merely his way of life. How he'd grown up. It was certainly how most of his set lived.

Hunter paused and turned about, sure he was being followed. Two, male, children's voices sounded behind him, and he turned again, this time catching the two little rascals who stopped and made an obvious attempt at looking at the sky.

"Do you have something you wish to ask me, boys?" he asked, walking up to them.

Their faces were not the cleanest, nor were their clothes well kept. Patches dotted the garments, obvious they'd been repaired many times over. One of the boys pant leg sat way too high on the lad's ankles. Certainly in this part of London they looked out of place.

This week he'd had several such episodes of children begging him for funds. Out the front of his home he was ambushed by a group of young boys, no more than eight years if a day, begging him for money, their grimy little faces and beseeching eyes ensuring he reached into his coat pocket to give them what they wanted.

He'd thought such an incident was unique, but he'd been wrong. On his return home from a ride in Hyde Park, he'd been accosted by a young woman, her gown was tidy, but she had an air of poverty that dulled her cheeks and eyes. She'd begged him for money to help pay for food for the children she had in her care. Again, he'd reached into his pocket and with nothing but a sovereign, had handed over the coin, granting her a boon she'd likely never see again.

The next few days had passed without incident, but now again, here he was being asked for charity. Never in his life had he been such a target and it truly was becoming absurd. One did not see beggars in Mayfair and St. James.

"Well, boys? What is it that you want?" Although he could guess easily enough.

They stared at him before flicking each other a glance. "We're looking for donations, my lord. To help with our school."

"Your school?" It hadn't been a word he'd heard so far with the other children looking for cash and the word *school* caught his attention. "You are being taught someplace." Hunter narrowed his eyes, curious and starting to see a pattern to all this accosting.

"Spitalfields Orphanage and School. We're raising funds so we can purchase a new building for children in the Ludgate area of the city. Us kids need a lot of help to make a go of it, sir. Help from men like you."

"You certainly do speak as though you've been taught reasonably well." A knowing feeling lodged in the pit of his stomach. "Tell me, who is your patron of the school. So I know where to send a donation."

"Miss Cecilia Smith, my lord."

The older boy whacked the younger one in the stomach, glaring at him. "Ye weren't meant to tell the toff anything, just to get a donation."

Why did it not surprise him... Hunter fought not to roll his eyes. The woman was a minx, a busybody who was now sending her students to ask for funds from a gentleman in Mayfair. He pulled out of his pocket a gold coin and tossed it in the air. As quick as a flash the elder boy's hand reached out and snatched it.

"Make sure Miss Smith receives the donation. And pray tell her, it is all she'll be receiving from me so she can stop sending her charges to do her dirty work."

The boys ran off, laughing and smiling, no doubt at their good fortune at gaining some funds just as their patron had said.

Hunter turned about and headed to Whites. The betting book always had good juicy wagers to lay some funds on, and he wouldn't get the opportunity again to check the log as he was headed to his good friends, Hamish Doherty, Earl Leighton's this evening for a ball.

His steps slowed as he walked along St James Street, the thought of Miss Smith bombarding his mind. What would she think of how he had managed her tricks? Would she be infuriated, challenged? Would her cheeks flush a becoming pink and her eyes sparkled with righteous fire at once again being denied? Suddenly, inexplicably, he could imagine how beautiful she would look in the latest cut and style of gown. A gown that would hug her breasts, and float about her long, thin legs hinting and teasing at what lay beneath. Her hair pulled high, showcasing her elegant neck and perfect profile. Any colour other than the drab grey he'd seen her wearing to date would set off her creamy complexion that looked un-kissed by the sun. A part of him hoped he would see her again. Even if he had to endure another set down, no matter how nicely worded she put them.

I want her. He faltered momentarily at the awareness. Should he wish her to be his mistress, maybe he ought to gain favour by visiting her charity, seeing for himself how she helped and what she did for these unfortunates of London.

Turning about, he looked to where the boys had scurried off to, but they were long gone. Where was it they said they were from again? Hunter started back the way he came and hailed a hackney.

"To Spitalfields Orphanage and school, and quickly."

CHAPTER 4

"I cannot find the box with the new chalkboards, Darcy, do you know where Katherine placed them?" Cecilia asked, wiping a loose strand of hair from her face. All day they'd searched for the missing chalkboards for the children who had just started at the school this week. And with Katherine out with her father in the country regarding a building job, Cecilia had not been able to ask where she'd placed them.

"Lord Aaron, what brings you here?"

Cecilia stopped looking through the cupboard that sat behind a large, reception desk that Darcy, the Duchess of Athelby was too standing behind. The marquess was here? Oh dear lord, that means he'd found out she was behind the children who she'd sent to pester him for funds for their charity. *Damn it.*

She stood, and made her presence known. The Marquess's attention snapped to her, but this time there was no amusement in his gaze, merely indifference. How changeable the man was.

"You know Miss Smith, Duchess?" he asked, not taking his gaze off Cecilia.

Darcy came over and took Cecilia's hand, pulling her over to where his lordship stood. "We've been friends these past twelve months. Our friendship was formed when I joined the London Relief Society, which of course Cecilia runs. I will do anything, as you well know, to help those less fortunate."

Cecilia bobbed a small curtsy. "Can we help you with anything, Lord Aaron?"

He gestured to a room off the side of the front office in which they stood. "I was accosted in the street by two little scamps who hail from this location. Asking for funds on St James Street mind you. This I believe was the fourth instance this week. I've come to suggest you keep a closer eye on those who explain they're under your care and charge."

Darcy grinned and patted Cecilia on the arm. "I think I'll leave you to deal with our delightful friend." She came around the desk and kissed the Marquess's cheek. "Come for dinner this week. We'd love to see you."

Cecilia ignored the stab of jealousy at seeing Darcy kiss a man who she had started to think about more than she ought. The past week she'd been endlessly thinking whether she'd see him again. Wondering if he'd figure out she was the one behind the children begging him for help and come to seek her out, just as he had done now. Cecilia had initially hoped he'd be so annoyed he would want to be rid of her, sell her the property and never see her again, but the thought gave her pause. To think she wouldn't get to verbally spar with Lord Aaron again left her feeling a little lost and disappointed.

She came and stood before him, and again was reminded of how very tall he was. She wasn't a short woman, and normally towered over men, so it was nice, in an exasperating kind of way that he peered down at her.

"Will you not answer my charge, Miss Smith."

"I don't know what you mean," she said, feigning any knowledge of his accusation. "None of our students would dare interrupt or intrude on a very busy and important marquess's affairs. Certainly not on St James's street where the famous Whites' Club is located. How very rude of two young boys to stop you from having your cigars and brandy with men of your ilk, where you'll discuss horses, money and what else is it that you discuss?" she said, forcing the most interested visage she could manage considering she had, in a roundabout way, just insulted the lord.

He stared at her a moment before his eyes narrowed just the slightest. She smiled.

"The boys said they were from this establishment and after our meeting yesterday I can only assume you mean to annoy me with your students until I gave way and sell you my building."

"You could just donate it to us. That would be even better."

"You are, Miss Smith, the most vexing woman I've ever met. I shall not be gifting you the building, now or ever, I can promise you that. I'd also like to ensure that your little scamps do not harass me again." He came around the front desk and stood not an inch from her person.

"I've also noted you're very apt at throwing out the insults to my sphere of Society. Are you jealous, by chance?" Lord Aaron asked.

"Of you and your friends? Well of course, my lord. I long for the days that a woman of a lower class will save my pitiful self on the street because I'm too drunk to see vehicles that are barrelling toward me."

He scoffed, a little muscle in his jaw flexed. "It is only expected that you would find my Society a little daunting since your rank is well beneath mine, and nights of enjoyment such as I endure would not suit you, I think. You're too clouded by your judgements, and would undoubtedly find such entertainments silly and beneath your moral notice. Why I'm surprised you lower yourself to speak to the Duchess of Athelby. However do you manage to do that?"

A peculiar and quite unfamiliar ache pierced her heart. "The duchess is a good woman, and helps those in need, unlike so many of your ilk, including yourself. As for your comment regarding your social sphere, are you saying that I could not hold my own if I attended one of your higher Society's balls?" How dare he imply such a thing. He was baiting her, she knew it, but it didn't change the fact that his words pricked her pride. She'd once longed to be able to attend such dinners and parties. Her own Society was lovely, and she'd grown rather fond of it, but a ball in the *ton*, where jewels and gowns were of the latest fashion, and everyone was free from working restraints, well, she couldn't help but want to see it. If only once.

He leaned closer still, and she caught the scent of mint on his breath. Annoyingly her gaze took in his mouth, his lips appeared soft and well looked after, not chafed or cracked from lack of good food and living. His hand reached out and slid along the desk, trapping her partly within his hold.

"If the slipper fits, Miss Smith."

She met his gaze and glared all the while her body fought for control. He was so close, so large and everything a gentleman of his ilk should be. Strong, intelligent, cutting and witty. A gentleman who seemed to have the uncanny knack to get under her skin. Not many did, but the marquess seemed to be apt at it.

She stepped back. "Since you're here my lord, and you have been most generous with your donations this past week, maybe you'd care for a tour. I can show you the classrooms and where the children sleep if you like. Maybe you'll find the organ that's within your chest wall, and sell to me after all."

He glanced about the foyer, his eyes flicking to the staircase where two little girls chuckled and ran off when spied.

"Lead the way, Miss Smith," he said, holding out his arm for her to take.

Well, she hadn't wished to link her arm with his, and she realized her mistake as soon as she did it. A jolt of awareness shot through her, and she took a calming breath to quiet her racing heart. Cecilia made the tour as short as possible, showing him the varied classrooms which they had in order of age, not gender. The less time she had to be touching him the better. They headed upstairs to where the children slept, their beds, rows after rows, showcasing just how many were in need of help.

"There are so many beds." The marquess frowned, halting at the sleeping quarter doors. "How many schools such as this one do you run, Miss Smith?"

"I have three in London, and one in the country. Of course, the number would grow should I purchase a property in Ludgate as planned."

He nodded but did not venture to enter the room. "I did not know there were so many in need."

Cecilia met his gaze, hearing the surprise in his voice that rang with truth. "A lot of people do not, but it is as you see. A growing problem, and one that I fear I shall never see fixed." They stood there for a couple of minutes, before heading back downstairs.

The duchess bustled into the room, carrying a box, no doubt the missing chalkboards they'd been searching for the past several hours. "I have decided to invite Miss Smith to the ball the duke and I are hosting Saturday next."

Cecilia moved to stand behind the reception desk, her chest tightening at the thought. "I cannot possibly attend your ball, your grace. It wouldn't be correct."

"Correct? La, half of those in attendance have less class than you, my dear and I do not care what anyone of my sphere thinks. You're my friend, we do charity work together, and I wish for you to be there with me. I will not accept any answer from you, but yes."

Cecilia's stomach roiled at the idea of all those people, women who could cut her dead in Society, people looking at her as a second-class citizen simply due to the fact her father worked for a living, didn't inherit it like all those who would be around her. But then, she was friends with the duchess and never felt belittled or looked down upon when with her, so maybe she was a little prejudiced against his lordship's social sphere. And she would not allow the marquess to think she could not attend because she was scared of how she would be treated by his kind. She had nothing to prove to them, if anything, they were the ones lacking in morals.

"Well then, it's a yes." She met his lordship's eye. "You see, Lord Aaron, since you viewed a little of my life, I will now get to view a little of yours. I look forward to seeing you at the ball."

He bowed and started for the door. "Alas, Miss Smith, I do believe I'm otherwise engaged that evening."

Cecilia glared at his back as he walked out the door. She didn't bother to reply, merely ripped open the box that held the chalkboards and pretended it was his lordship's head.

CHAPTER 5

S till smarting from the rude and inappropriate remark from Lord Aaron the week before, Cecilia had thrown herself into her charities and helping her father prepare for court. It left little time for her to dwell on his parting words. How was she to convince him to sell the property if he wasn't in attendance at the ball?

The duchess had said he would be, but until Cecilia saw him with her own eyes, the doubt he would not attend festered.

The young woman she'd hired to help her with her hair placed the last pin in the fashionable and pretty design. Tonight her hair was completely up, but the curls were large and soft looking. A strand of her mother's pearls threaded throughout the design. They may not be rubies or diamonds as so many of the women of the social sphere she was about to enter wore, but they did well enough and at least gave her an air of wealth, even if she did have the stench of trade floating about her silk slippers.

"You look beautiful, my dear. Stand and let me look at

you." Her mother bustled into the room and took her hands, making her stand.

Cecilia twirled for good measure and laughed when her mother dabbed at her eyes.

"It's only a ball, mother. I'm not getting married." She walked over to her bed and slid the soft pink slippers on that matched the dress she'd been lucky enough to find only a few days ago on Cannon Street. The gown had been made for a woman of means, but then when she'd gone to collect the garment, she'd disliked the colour against her skin and refused to take it. The modiste, Madame Perrin was only too happy to give her a small discount if Cecilia would take the dress, and lucky for her, the gown had suited her complexion perfectly, and was suitable without being too fancy.

"Even so, you look so lovely. How wonderful for the Duchess of Athelby to invite you as her special guest. I do hope you'll remember to be polite and try and not let anyone vex you."

Cecilia pulled on her white silk gloves. "I won't pretend to not understand what you're saying, because I do perfectly well. But I promise I shall behave myself, and not allow my mouth to run away from me and tell off all the rich nobs or at least tell them what I truly think of their shallowness. Will that suffice, mama?"

"Now now, you cannot tarnish everyone the same. Some of those in attendance will be just like you, not full of airs and graces, just attending for the enjoyment of fine food, music and dancing. Oh, I do hope I can stay up to hear all about it, but alas no doubt you will not return until the wee hours of the morning."

"I should think so, but do not wait up mama. I'll tell you everything tomorrow at breakfast." Cecilia pulled on her cloak and started for the door. "Now, I must be off. I think I just heard our carriage pull up."

"Have fun, my dear!"

Cecilia chuckled as she made her way outside to the carriage. Well, if she didn't have fun, at least it was a memory that she could keep for the rest of her life. She could say to her children that she once danced and was merry with the haute *ton*. Not everyone could boast such a triumph.

HUNTER NURSED A GLASS OF WHISKY, the amber liquid quenched his thirst, but only for a short time. He needed many more of these tonight if he were to survive it. His nemesis, Miss Smith, stood next to the Duke and Duchess of Athelby and was talking to a fellow Hunter hadn't seen in town for two years or more. The gentleman's name eluded him at present. Who was the blasted flirt?

He took another good sip and blinked to clear his eyes. He'd not intended to attend this evening, certainly not after hearing Miss Smith was invited, but the allure of a pair of very pretty blue eyes changed his plans. Miss Smith was certainly looking very well this evening, the rose pink of her gown suited her fair complexion and long blonde locks, that were arranged atop her head. He had to admit, the hell cat almost looked like one of them, but every now and then something would catch her eye, and the disdain she carried for his lot in life was visible to his inspection.

Hunter sighed and started toward the card room, but his feet, a little more unsteady than he'd believed only got as far as some empty chairs and he sat down, gesturing to a footman to bring him more of that delightful amber liquid.

How long he sat there, lost in his own thoughts was anyone's guess, so when a vision in pink sat beside him, he was startled when she spoke.

"You're foxed, Lord Aaron. Please tell me I'm not going to have to rescue you tonight as well. I don't think these silk slippers would survive the London streets."

He harrumphed. "I need no rescuing, and least of all from you." He frowned at his cutting words that he didn't mean to be so abrupt. But Miss Smith had a way of annoying him greatly, and the fact that tonight she looked more becoming than anyone he'd ever met before only made the situation worse. She was common for crying out loud. No better than the maids who worked in his homes. Well, maybe a little above his employees, but not by much. She took care of everyone, always sought to make people's lives better, whereas he thought of little other than himself, how to enjoy life as much as he could. His parents had certainly lived in such a way, and no harm ever came of it.

A little voice reminded Hunter that no good came from it either.

"Do you get so very drunk all the time, my lord?"

The footman delivered his drink and he took a sip. "Being from the Society that you are, I'll forgive your crass behaviour and give you a little lesson in manners. You never, ever ask a gentleman if he is foxed at any event he attends. You never ask at all. It is no one's concern but mine, and as I'm unwed, and nor am I engaged, I shall do whatever the bloody hell I want."

If he'd expected his words to send her packing, he was greatly disappointed. Miss vexing Smith simply narrowed her eyes at him and wrenched the whisky glass from his hand.

"You are making a spectacle of yourself. Twice now

I've had the unfortunate pleasure of seeing you in such a state. Do you never attend a ball where you're sober? You know if you tried it, you might actually enjoy it."

"I doubt it very much," he said, taking back the glass and finishing it. His eyes watered and he rubbed them, blinking a little to try and clear his vision. Miss Smith was starting to look like a blurry mound of pink.

"You do realize that if you sold me the building, I will leave you alone. I promise never to enter your Society again and will never seek you out as I have done so this evening. So, what say you? Are you willing to reconsider my proposal?"

He blinked again, wanting to see her clearly. Hell, she was pretty, ethereal almost, her features soft, delicate and perfectly structured. Until her eyes that was. They were intelligent, calculating and right at this moment, judgemental. It stung when it shouldn't have, for he did not care about her opinion. Or did he? Hunter frowned, not understanding the unknown disquiet stirring inside.

"No matter what you think of me, Miss Smith, let this be known. I may be a lord, but I do enjoy business, such as buying and selling horse stock, estates that I've inherited but do not use, the building on Pilgrim Street being one of them. But in this instance, as I have explained, I wish to develop it into a gentleman's club, not ruin an area that is improving as a location which should increase in value. It will decrease in value if that site is turned into an orphanage. That would never equate to good business."

She shifted on the chair beside him and met his gaze, her angelic features hard with loathing. Loathing for him. Damn, he didn't like that look on her. He wanted her to look at him with anything but that. Sweetness, heat, passion, anything but contempt.

"You're an embarrassment to Society, *my lord*. At least I'm trying to better the world for those who are less fortunate. What do you do?"

"You're so intelligent, why don't you tell me?" he said, wanting to mock her words as, damn it, they stung. The images of the needy children who'd begged him for money bombarded his mind, and he frowned. Was he an embarrassment? An uncaring, toff. Surely not, it was simply his way of life. He did not deny those who begged him, and over the years he'd instructed his man of affairs to donate to charities when his patronage had been sought.

"You do nothing other than drink yourself into a stupor and make money with your ventures, and yet all around you people live in poverty. At least I can sleep at night knowing I've done my best. You, my esteemed lord, are a parasite."

She stood, and he watched her go. His jaw ached, and he summoned another glass of whisky to dispel his annoyance. What did she know anyway? Who was she to criticise him for how he lived his life.

Hunter stood and started for the card room. He would dispel his frustrations in a game of cards. Better that than strangling the little middle class, righteous heathen in front of all the *ton*.

The card room was full of men, like him no doubt trying to escape the fairer sex or looking for a diversion from them. He spied the Duke of Athelby who had joined a game, and sat himself down at his table, willing to wait for him to be able to join in.

The duke, Cameron to his friends, threw him an amused glance. "What's got you all flustered? You look like you've danced every reel since the beginning of the ball."

Did he look like he'd been dancing like a popinjay? He

shook his head and summoned a glass of brandy from a passing footman. "The vexing woman that your wife brought if you must know. Right now, I have no doubt she's telling your wife that I'm greedy and have no heart, just as she implied to my face five minutes ago."

The duke choked on his wine, and Lord Nash seated across from Hunter bellowed out a God almighty laugh, bringing to attention their table.

"She did what?" Cameron asked, putting his card playing aside for a moment.

"Told me I'm a parasite because I do not help charities like the one she runs, with the help of your wife I might add."

Cameron smirked. "Darcy likes her. She thinks she's intelligent and kind, more than a lot of those in attendance this evening. No offence to you, Lord Nash, of course," the duke said, smiling.

Lord Nash nodded but didn't comment, merely studied his cards. Hunter took a long pull of his drink. "Even so, she does not suit this environment. She is not one of us. Does not fit in. Admit it, Cameron, even you wouldn't lower yourself to talk to her had your wife not made you."

The duke frowned, this time placing his cards down and levelled his gaze on Hunter. "I've known Miss Smith for some years, longer than I've known you, in fact. I use her father's firm for all my legal matters. They may have ink stains on their fingers, but they're very respectable people. And Cecilia is beyond intelligent, even Darcy admitted the other day that she thought Cecilia was more intelligent than her, and that's a rarity." The duke laughed, picking up his cards. "By the way, how sober are you at the moment? I don't want an unjust advantage against you in cards. I always find winning under such circumstances tedious."

Hunter looked down at the empty glass in his hand and waved to the footman for another. "Not foxed enough if anything. Not if I have to put up with middle class hell cats who call me a parasite."

"You are not a parasite, merely misunderstood perhaps or even, not aware so much of what goes on about us outside of Mayfair. I know from Darcy's charity work that I've become more in tune to the poverty people live with. Miss Smith wants you to sell her your building, I think she's showing you her strong opinions regarding the poor, merely to change your mind. I don't believe she means to be cutting or judgemental."

Hunter fought not to scoff. Miss Smith was the most judgemental woman he knew, no matter what Cameron said about the fact. "I am not blind to the poor, I just choose to live without it dictating my every move." The thought sounded uncaring even to Hunter's own ears, and he cringed.

"You're acting as I used to, dear fellow. Like the world should pander to your every wish and desire. Be pretty and correct, not ugly and poor, rough about the edges. Not everyone in London are as fortunate as us. As human beings, we accept this and remain polite, help when we can. I hope you've remained polite to Miss Smith. She does not deserve your cutting words."

Hunter took the drink from the footman and revelled in the sharp scent of brandy. "I was honest with her."

"You were rude, admit it. And now I shall have Darcy onto me about how my friend was rude to hers."

"Darcy is my friend too."

"She won't be after tonight if she finds out you were a prig."

Hunter downed his drink, and the room spun for a

moment. "There was a time when you were a very good prig."

"Just sell her the building, and your troubles with Miss Smith will disappear."

Hunter ran a hand through his hair and leaned back in the chair, no longer looking to play a game of cards. Not here at least. Maybe he'd go to Whites later tonight, and anywhere else the night may take him.

"I have plans afoot on the location for a gentleman's club for bankers and lawyers, men of that calibre. Miss Smith thinks my idea foolish, but I digress, I think it's an untapped money-making venture I want to get started as soon as may be." A flash of pink caught his eye, and he turned to see Darcy and the very woman who vexed him greatly come to stand before them.

Miss Smith curtsied as the duke, and regretfully, Hunter stood to greet them. The duke took Darcy's hand and placed it on his arm, covering it with his as they glanced at each other. A year after their marriage and the pair were still madly in love. As much as Hunter was happy for them, it was also too, a little confronting. He'd grown up in a household where love was folly, fun and games, and not always with your spouse was the tone, not all this affection and fidelity. Hunter wasn't sure what to make of them, or the fact that the duke and duchess made a mockery of his parents' marriage every day. Made a mockery of what he'd always thought as normal in a marriage.

"I've come to steal my husband away for a dance."

Hunter glanced at Miss Smith and smarted at the look of horror that crossed the woman's face. No doubt being left alone with him and his Society left her horrified.

"Lord Aaron, will you do the honour of dancing with our guest, Miss Smith. We would be very pleased if you would," the duchess said, smiling at them both.

"Do not feel that because I accompanied her grace here that I was looking for a dance partner, Lord Aaron." She turned to the duke and duchess. "I shall return to the ballroom and meet up with you after the waltz."

Before the duchess had a chance of reply, Miss Smith turned on her heel and headed back toward the ballroom. Darcy turned her steely gaze on him, and he groaned.

"Hunter, follow Miss Smith and ask her to dance," the duchess said, glaring at him.

"It's obvious she does not care to dance with me." He snatched another glass of whisky from a passing footman. "I do not wish to force her hand."

Just as quick as he'd claimed the drink, Darcy snatched it out of his hands. "I think you've had enough liquor tonight. Now go, and ask her, and be kind or you shall have me to deal with."

He raised his brow at the duchess and instead of arguing the point, which damn it, she probably had an argument for, he headed into the ballroom to seek out Miss Smith.

He saw her nestled in one of the corners, her height making her easy to find. Some rather large and boisterous matrons stood before her and gave him a sharp look when he asked to move past them.

Cecilia too looked at him with contempt, and he tampered down his annoyance and held out his hand.

"Would you care to dance, Miss Smith? I do believe the next song is to be a waltz."

"I do not," she said, crossing her arms and looking over his shoulder.

He took her hand anyway and pulled her toward the dance floor. Hunter cringed as she tightened her hold, stabbing him with her fingernails. What did she have in her gloves, little knives?

"That hurts, Miss Smith."

She swung into his arms, fitting him like a glove. He liked that, and what's more, he liked the feel of her in his hold. Her silk gown slid against his palms, her hand fit perfectly within his, her waist was small and yet still held delectable womanly curves he adored.

"I never do anything without a purpose, Lord Aaron."

He chuckled and steered them down the ballroom floor. "I think we shall enjoy the dance more if we suffer our time together in silence. Are you in agreement, Miss Smith?"

Her crystal clear eyes, unlike his which had a tendency to see things a little blurry most nights narrowed slightly. "I fail to care if we converse or not, but I will tell you this, your breath reeks of whisky, and if you step on my feet again I will retaliate in kind."

Pox on her for insinuating he was foxed. "Maybe you ought to stop breathing then?" He smiled at her shock and then swore when her slippered foot, something that had looked delicate slammed down on his toes.

☙❧

CECILIA STOOD in the middle of the ballroom and waited for Lord Aaron to regain his composure. Gentleman had their feet stepped on often and so too did women, why he had wrenched her out of his arms while he inspected his injured toe was simply embarrassing. And not for her.

"Is your toe well, my lord. I do apologise. I certainly didn't mean to be so clumsy on purpose." Cecilia smiled at the haute *ton* who looked on, some down their pointed noses, but Cecilia simply allowed their censure to roll off her back. What did it matter what these people thought? Outside of these walls, the majority of them didn't worry about anyone else except their own person or families. Cecilia could count on one hand how many she knew here who worked for her charity or those that worked for other charities like hers.

It was a pitiful few, and the dandy who kneeled before her, inspecting his toe, which she was surprised he could feel at all since he was so drunk, was simply absurd. This was the fourth time she'd been in his lordship's company and the second time she'd seen his glassy, unfocused eyes, not to mention his unsteady gait, although he seemed quite apt at hiding that a lot of the time.

But she didn't miss the slowing of steps to regain one's balance, or the shaking of his hands when he drank, or that the trembling ceased a little once he'd imbibed himself of that liquor. The man was a drunk. Unfortunately, Cecilia had seen many like him, fathers, mothers, carers of the children she dealt with daily. Most of the time the children chose to stay at her institutions on their own accord simply to stay alive.

He stood and pulled her into his arms, twirling them once again into the fray of dancers as if nothing was amiss. Did no one see this man? Did no one know the troubles he fought within his outer visage?

"All is well again, my lord?"

"Yes, it shall be," he said, flicking her a glance that spoke of annoyance more than anything else.

"While I have your ear, tell me, have you thought more on my offer? I do hope you've realised by now that the amount we're willing to pay is reasonable and my idea for the location is more suited for that part of London."

"The property is not for sale, Miss Smith."

His stoic and no-nonsense tone said more than anything that he was at an end with her trying to make him sell. "It doesn't matter anymore anyway. We've found

45

another building for sale, right next door to yours. So even if you refurbish your building to a be a gentleman's club, I'll ensure no one will want to go there simply because of who your neighbours are."

He didn't look at her, merely continued to look bored. "Gentleman will still come, no matter how much you try and sabotage me."

He was the most vexing man she'd ever met.

The dance continued on for a few more minutes, but by the time it came to an end, Cecilia had well and truly had enough being around Lord Aaron and his friends. Cecilia thanked him for the dance, curtsied and sought out the Duchess of Athelby. It was time she returned home in any case. She had an appointment at lunch to look over the paperwork for their new location, and she needed to have her wits about her.

She found the duke and duchess speaking privately, but Darcy as she knew her by when alone, smiled as she came closer and didn't reject her company. "Did you enjoy your dance, Cecilia?" the duchess asked, looking past her, no doubt trying to locate Lord Aaron who was nowhere to be found. Thankfully.

"I did, thank you, but I must return home. As you know I'm looking at the new building we've found tomorrow, and I want to be refreshed and ready for my meeting."

"Did you wish for me to attend? I admit I do not know much about contracts and what is legal, but having a duchess there could be beneficial if the vendor starts to increase his price or some such nonsense."

"No, that shall not be necessary. My father's business partner, Mr. White will be in attendance with me and will ensure all runs smoothly."

The duchess' lips flattened. "Mr. White is going to be there? In that case, I shall be in attendance."

"Why so, my dear?" the duke asked, looking down at his wife, a small frown line between his otherwise perfect brows.

"Mr. White wishes to marry Miss Smith, my dear. Has so for some time. A chaperone is necessary I think."

"Who wishes to marry Miss Smith?" Lord Aaron asked, coming to join them, with two glasses of whisky in hand. He caught her looking at them, and she didn't miss the reluctance when he handed one over to the duke. Like that was what he wanted to do. Ha. He didn't want to part with any of his fine wine or hard liquor if he didn't have to.

"Mr. White, Hunter. Not that we should be discussing such things, here and so openly. I do apologise, Miss Smith."

Cecilia could feel the heat start up her neck and tried to think of anything else other than the fact they were discussing her life and who wanted to be a part of it, if only she'd say yes.

"You're to be married, Miss Smith. Well, aren't you a sly fox. You didn't tell me the wonderful news."

"No, my lord, I did not. And the only thing around here resembling that animal is you. Now, if you'll excuse me." She turned to the duke and duchess. "Good night, your graces."

They bid her farewell, and she ignored the burning between her shoulders. Lord Aaron could try and intimidate her as much as he liked, but she wouldn't allow him to get the better of her. Unfortunately, she would have to make allowances to his lordship since he had a vice that seemed well and truly solidified in him. A man, who, unfortunately, was in his cups most of the time and did not and could not have his wits about him. A man who had learned to not care about anything other than his own self-worth.

Cecilia waited for the footman to collect her shawl and send for her carriage. She sighed in relief. At least that should be the final time she would have to deal with Lord Aaron.

CHAPTER 6

The offices of J Smith and Sons were busy today with in chambers work for upcoming court cases. Cecilia walked into the office her father had gifted her, not only to help him with matters pertaining to law but to have someplace other than their home to work on her charities.

The office had a delightful view of the footpath outside, and she sat behind her desk a moment to enjoy her solitude and her own little space. She'd always loved the room and most of all that her father had given her wall to wall bookshelves for anything she wanted to fill them with.

A light knock on the door sounded, and Mr. White peeked around the threshold, smiling in welcome.

Cecilia pasted on a polite visage and bade him enter, not that she wanted to go over the paperwork for the new location they'd found, and certainly not with him. There was a time when she had liked Mr. White, counted him as a friend, but not anymore. His advances since her father had given him leave to court her had sometimes gone beyond acceptable, and he seemed to think he had the right to touch her person, even clasping her hand to place on his arm or to touch the small of her back. Neither of which she wanted him to do, now or ever. Her objections did not seem to deter the man, and that lowered her estimation of him even further.

"Mr. White, thank you for helping me with these contracts. Please, do be seated. We'll go over them before we head down to Pilgrim Street to look through the building with the vendor."

He sat, his oiled hair slicked severely back made him look like a raven. Pity he wasn't as smart as one of those birds, certainly not when it came to women at least.

"My pleasure, Cecilia, and let me say how fetching you look today. Is that a new gown?"

Cecilia looked down at her drab, brown dress that had no feminine features on it other than the fact it was a dress. She didn't like to wear her best gowns when she came into the office, preferring to be comfortable over fashionable. "Thank you for the compliment, but as this is work, we should probably forget about our clothing and discuss the matter at hand. The purchase, remember?"

"Ah yes, now, I have been thinking over the matter. Your father gave me the contract to look over on the weekend, and while everything within it looks fine, I do not believe it would be a sound investment for your charity." He leaned back in his chair, pulling out a cheroot from his coat pocket and proceeded to light it using the candle that sat burning on her desk.

"Please enlighten me as to why you've come to that conclusion?" The building was solid, not damaged or needing major repairs. The interior, of course, needed full refurbishment and upgrading to house the school and dorms for the children, but that wasn't anything they'd not attempted and completed before in other areas of London.

"A woman of your age should be looking to other things to occupy her time. Like marrying, starting a family, looking after the offspring of her own, not worrying about the poor of London. Who, I might add, will take advantage of your charity and then proceed to do nothing at all with the education you give them. I see such expenditure as a waste of time."

Cecilia stood and made her way to the door, picking up her shawl. "Pick up the papers on the desk and follow me. I don't wish to be late for my appointment." She walked from the room, her teeth clenched tightly closed lest she turnabout and tell this buffoon exactly what she thought of him. How dare he even suggest helping others was a waste of time. The pompous fool had not an ounce of empathy in his body.

What was with the gentlemen of her acquaintance who all seemed to think charity was a waste of time. Was she the only one who cared, who had sympathy?

Cecilia ripped open the carriage door and jumped up into the firm's coach and waited for Mr. White. He soon followed her out and into the vehicle, seating himself next to her instead of taking the seat across. A welcome reprieve from having to occasionally look at him during the journey.

"I did not mean to offend you, Cecilia, but I was talking to your father, and he agrees. This kind of lifestyle you're leading is not becoming of a lady." He paused, pulling at his neckcloth before he met her gaze. "Have you thought any more on the prospect of us marrying? If you agreed, we could be married within a month or so. I know I for one would wish for this very much."

Cecilia held his gaze and for what felt like the hundredth time, picked her words wisely lest she offended the silly man who did not understand the word no.

"Mr. White while you're an honourable gentleman I must repeat what I've said already to you. We would not suit and as sorry as I am to hurt you, my answer regarding your proposal is no. Please do not make our acquaintance any more awkward than it already is by asking again."

He clasped her hand, kissing it with an absurd amount of embellishment. Cecilia stilled and tried to pry her hand free without success. "Mr. White let go of my hand."

"Marry me, Cecilia. I want nothing but to pleasure you in all ways. Let me love you as a husband should love a wife. Perhaps if you allowed yourself to kiss me, you may see I am the man for you, that we would suit."

She tried to wrench free, and it was like trying to pull her hand from s*tone*. "I apologise, but I do not see you in a romantic way, sir."

He lunged, an ominous sound if ever there was one, before he pushed her up against the squabs, trapping her there. His disgusting, sloppy mouth took hers, and she gasped. The action was the worst thing she could have done, as he took advantage of the fact and kissed her deeply, more deeply than she'd ever been kissed before.

Vaguely she felt the carriage rock to a halt, all the while she fought to get him off her person. She couldn't breathe, and panic started to rise in her stomach. What if he didn't stop. What if he…

Cecilia heard the carriage door open and watched as the Marquess of Aaron ripped Mr. White from her, pulled the man through the door and throw him most unceremoniously onto the footpath.

For a moment she sat there, trying to regain her composure. Her blood pounded in her ears, her breathing erratic and sitting up, she clutched her hands together to stop them from shaking.

"Miss Smith, are you well?"

The voice, deep, cultured and one filled with concern lulled her from her shock.

"Miss Smith?" he asked again.

Cecilia turned toward Lord Aaron who studied her in a way she'd never seen before. He actually appeared genuinely concerned. She nodded, and a curl dropped beside her cheek. Reaching up she tried to amend her hair which had been terribly dishevelled during her scuffle with Mr. White. Oh dear lord, what would the marquess think of her?

"I am well." She turned to his lordship and spied Mr. White standing aside from the duchess, his cheeks flushed red. "Thank you for removing, for helping me to remove..."

"You're welcome, come," he said, holding out his hand. "I accompanied the duchess today as she insisted she be here for the inspection and the duke was unable to escort her. I would say after what I just witnessed that it was a good thing we did come."

Cecilia nodded, giving his lordship her hand as he helped her step down. "Are you not angry that we're inspecting the building right next to yours, my lord? I hope you're not here to outbid me on the property."

"I am not here for that, I do have an alternate reason for coming."

"And that is?" she asked, not sure she was fully comfortable with the caring, sober marquess. When he was like this, he was likeable and more handsome than she liked to admit.

"To apologise for my treatment of you the other evening. I was harsh and unkind, and I'm sorry for that."

Lost for words, his lordship placed her hand on his

arm, gesturing for the duchess to start toward their intended location. "But before we go any further there is a matter I need to address." He came up to where Mr. White was standing and stopped. "Go ahead, Miss Smith. I will join you and the duchess shortly." Cecilia did as he bade and came up to Darcy, who took her hand in support.

From where they stood Cecilia couldn't hear what the marquess was saying to Mr. White, but whatever it was the man's cheeks turned a darker crimson with every word. The marquess made Mr. White appear small, and he was a tall man himself. Cecilia couldn't help but take in the marquess's appearance and revel in it a little. For all his vices and opinions, he was dastardly good looking. A hell-raising rake.

Mr. White looked over at her, glaring, and she refused to back down to his bullying and look away. How dare he try and make her feel like she'd done something wrong? When she returned home, she would inform her father of his inappropriate conduct in the carriage and have the leech fired.

The Marquess stood back gesturing to the carriage, and Mr. White stepped inside, and before long the carriage was gone, and Cecilia and the duchess were left with his lordship. A gentleman came toward them on the footpath and waved as he came closer.

"Miss Smith, how very sorry I am for being late. I was held up at the office." He held out his hand, and Cecilia shook it.

"This is the Marquess of Aaron and the Duchess of Athelby, Mr. Conners." Cecilia made the introductions, and comically the older gentleman's mouth popped open and couldn't form words for a moment. She supposed it wasn't every day that the lawyer would meet such people of high rank.

Their tour of the building was brief as most of the interior was the same, run down and dark. It did have potential, but would cost more to repair than Cecilia's first choice. There was plenty of room for sleeping quarters and large enough that the school could be kept separate from those areas. Cecilia clasped her hands before her, trying to stem their shaking. She would not let her altercation with Mr. White dampen her inspection of this site.

The duchess had moved into another area of the building with Mr. Conners, and Cecilia found herself alone with the marquess. Quite alone and in quite a dark little room, maybe a storeroom at one time. Unlike when she was trapped in the carriage with Mr. White, her stomach didn't have a ball of uneasiness lodged within it, if anything, she felt protected and safe. How strange, but also perplexingly wonderful.

"I still think my building is a much better option," the marques said, taking out a silver flask and having a small sip.

"Have you changed your mind? I would purchase that one if only you weren't such a greedy little lord," she said, grinning a little to temper her words.

He chuckled, and a devilish light flickered in his cobalt coloured eyes. "There is nothing little about me, Miss Smith."

She rolled her eyes and fought not to blush. The man had no shame. "Self- praise is never a virtue, my lord." Cecilia chuckled and walked to a nearby window, looking over the street below.

His footsteps sounded behind her, coming to a halt near her back. "Did he hurt you?"

Although he didn't ask who had hurt her, she understood who he meant. "He forcibly kissed me, wouldn't let me go. I shall speak to my father about his conduct. Mr.

White wishes to marry me, you see. I should amend, that is to say, he believes we will marry, it's just a matter of time."

"Will your father allow the gentleman to get away with such insult to your person. Do you wish for me to speak to him?"

Cecilia turned and met his gaze. "No, it'll be fine, I'm sure my father will deal with Mr. White severely and imme-diately upon my return."

"Has he tried to kiss you before?"

His lordship's gaze dropped to her mouth, and the most delicious shiver rolled about in her belly. Did the marquess wish to kiss her too? Was that what he was think-ing? *Oh, yes please.* He might vex her at every turn, but she'd rather have any other memory than that of Mr. White.

"He's shown little signs of ownership of me in front of his work colleagues and my father, but he's never tried to kiss me before. But then, we'd never been alone before."

"Like we are now."

Cecilia nodded. "Exactly, but I don't think I have anything to worry about with you, Lord Aaron. We are not what you would call friends or anything near lovers."

"Are we not?" he stepped closer still, and Cecilia caught the scent of sandalwood.

Oh dear, not only was he one of the most handsome men of her acquaintance, but he also smelt divine. Their eyes met and held. A shiver of expectation ran through her as he leaned toward her. Cecilia followed his lead, and at the last moment, before their lips touched, she closed her eyes.

The chatter of the duchess' voice sounded in the corridor outside and as slow as a cat, Lord Aaron stepped away as if nothing, in particular, had almost occurred between them. Cecilia took a calming breath, her blood thumping loud in her ears.

What was she thinking even contemplating allowing his lordship to kiss her? Especially here where they were not entirely alone. She watched him, and he cast a quick glance her way, and her stomach flipped at the unsated need that burned within his cobalt gaze.

"I think the charity should put in an offer, Cecilia. This will be the perfect location, and it's large enough with little structural things fixed on it, if I'm reading the report correctly that is. Of course, we'll have your father's law firm look over the contract, but I think it's quite perfect. What do you say?"

Cecilia couldn't agree more. "If father approves the contract we'll place an offer Mr. Conners. We'll be in contact again next week to let you know."

With their appointment completed, they made their way back outside. Cecilia cursed Mr. White as the fiend hadn't bothered to send the company carriage back for her. The carriage sporting the Marquess's emblem on its door sat parked beside the curb, the driver seated atop with a large whip in hand. "Allow us to escort you back home or to the offices, Miss Smith."

"Thank you, that is very kind," she said, taking his lordship's hand, and climbing up into the equipage.

Once seated, they pulled away and the duchess glanced at her. "I have an appointment with the duke that I cannot be late to. Do you think you could drop me off first, Lord Aaron? I know it isn't ideal, but we've spent longer than I thought we would at the building, and I'm now in danger of missing it."

"That is no trouble, I assure you." Lord Aaron turned toward where the driver sat and opened a little window inside the carriage and notified the driver of the change of direction. Closing it again he caught Cecilia's eye and her stomach clenched in that odd little way that only he seemed to bring forth.

"Are you comfortable with me taking you back home or to your office, Miss Smith? We shall be unchaperoned for a few minutes at least. I do not wish to injure your reputation."

"That will be fine, my lord." Within a few minutes, the carriage rocked to a halt outside the duchess' London home, and Cecilia couldn't help but look up at the massive, impressive Georgian structure and marvel at its size and the opulent wealth and power it portrayed to those looking in.

And yet, the duchess was a kind, honest woman who didn't see people for what material things they had. No, she had a solid moral code and surrounded herself with people who helped others before themselves. Cecilia supposed somewhere within the marquess he must have a heart beating and more common sense than what she'd been privy to if the duchess called him her friend.

Bidding the duchess goodbye the carriage pulled back out into the busy London traffic. "Did you wish to return to your father's offices or home, Miss Smith?"

"Actually, I'd prefer to return home. It's in Cheapside I'm afraid, so you'll be doubling back. I'll talk to papa about what happened today in privacy and without the possible interruption of Mr. White."

The marquess called out the change of direction and settled back in the squabs. He took out his flask and had a small sip before placing it back in his coat pocket. "The gentleman your father has as his successor is no gentleman at all. If you only ask, I shall ensure he's removed from your father's employ where he can never touch you again."

Cecilia sighed, if only it were that easy. "Father wishes

for me to marry him, and I suppose if he gets his way, Mr. White will be able to touch me whenever he wishes."

"Never say such words. The thought of him touching you makes my blood run cold."

The blood in her veins did the exact opposite. "I think you've been imbibing too much on that silver flask in your pocket, Lord Aaron," she said it with a tinge of amusement, but his statement was anything but funny. His lordship would never look to her as a possible wife, she was too bossy, too opinionated and most of all, too common. A man like Lord Aaron would expect her to become a lady of leisure, sew, paint and be at home so other ladies of similar standing could call and they could all discuss the mundane news of tonnish life.

But then, the duchess didn't live such an existence, she was involved with many charities and Cecilia had never heard her mention that she must be at home for appointments of that kind. So maybe life could be different... If he stopped drinking which by the looks of it would not stop anytime soon.

"No such thing. I may like my liquor, Miss Smith, but I still have my faculties, most of the time at least and I can assure you, seeing you married to Mr. White would not please me."

"Really," she said, raising one brow. "What would please you, my lord?" Did she really wish to know? His gaze met hers and the intent she read in his blue steely eyes would have made her weak in the knees had she been standing.

❧

HUNTER WATCHED AS MISS SMITH, Cecilia bit her bottom lip. He wanted to reach for his flask, soothe the hunger he had for the liquor almost every moment of every day, but he didn't. Another hunger rumbled within, one where he kissed the woman who sat across from him with abandon. Crush her lips against his and taste her sweet self that had haunted his dreams for days.

He leaned back against the squabs. "What an interesting question Miss Smith. What would please me? Do you really wish to know? You may not like what I say in return."

"I think I shall be able to handle your reply."

He shifted over to the seat beside her. Miss Smith merely raised her chin at his forward manner but didn't move away. "Last chance to deny me."

She shook her head. "No, I want to know. Please tell me," she said, breathlessly.

"I want…I want to kiss you, remove all trace of that god-awful thing that was molesting you when I opened your carriage door." His hand reached up, and he traced her bottom lip with his thumb. "So soft."

Her attention snapped to his lips. He had her now, and she was thinking possibly even imagining what it would be like to kiss him back.

"Do you think that would be a good idea? We're in the middle of London, anyone could see us and what we were doing in here."

Hunter quickly untied the carriage blinds and let them drop. Ensconced in privacy, he raised his brows, grinning. "Better, Miss Smith? Or are you too scared to kiss me."

"I'm not scared of anything, least of all you," she said, shuffling closer, clasping his jaw and kissing him just as he'd hoped.

For a moment he was stunned that she'd been the one to initiate the kiss, chaste as it was, but when she went to pull away, he put paid to that and wrenched her back. He'd wanted to kiss her for days now, and no way in hell would he leave today without tasting her. Her lips were soft, supple and kissing him with the expertise of a courtesan. For a moment he wondered where she'd learnt such skills before the light graze of her breasts against his chest made him lose all train of thought.

He ached with want of her, something he'd not experienced before, not even with his past mistresses. Her hand slid into his hair, tugged him closer still, and he didn't deny her. His tongue touched hers, tentative at first and within a moment she was kissing him with as much need, as much enthusiasm as he was. He would never get enough of her.

Her hairpins gave way, and her long golden locks fell about her shoulders. He wanted to wrench away, see what she looked like in such disarray, but he couldn't, no matter how much he tried.

The carriage rocked to a halt, and she drew away, her cheeks a pretty shade of pink, her eyes wide and full of revelation.

"I hope that hasn't scared you off, Miss Smith," he managed to say, clearing his throat when it sounded too heavy with need, too deep with want.

"On the contrary Lord Aaron, it's merely made me more curious."

Although her words rang with truth, Miss Smith did in fact bolt from the carriage and toward her front door which opened when she started up the stairs. Hunter watched her go, even if he wanted to follow her and see where that kiss could lead. He took out his flask and the scent of the whisky smelt less tempting. There was something much more delicious and damn it, it had disappeared into the house without even a backward glance.

He tapped his cane on the roof, and the carriage pulled away. Where would he see her again? Or better yet, how could he manage to get them together again without being obvious. He would write to the duchess on his return home and see if she had any plans of inviting Miss Smith to any more events.

And if not, well, he would just have to ensure he ran into her somewhere. And somewhere soon.

CHAPTER 7

Cecilia sat in her father's office at home, staring in disbelief as he chastised her for the atrocious behaviour she'd partaken in within the carriage the day before. For a moment, Cecilia had thought he'd learnt of her forwardness with Lord Aaron but was only slightly relieved to hear he was, in fact, talking about Mr. White.

"I was not at all in the wrong, papa. He forced me to kiss him. Something that has not, nor ever will interest me."

Her father leaned forward on his desk, clasping his hands together atop the parchment that lay before him. "He is a good match for you, my dear. He's also going to take over the business when I pass on. I would prefer that he marries someone in the family if only to keep the business in our hands. I would so hate for it to be lost."

Cecilia stood and paced in front of the windows. "Father, I do not love him, nor do I find him at all attractive and even less so now that he took the liberty to insult me when he had no right. I'll not put up with that from him or anyone else, and I'll not do as you ask. If you want the company to stay in the family hands, I suggest you have another child with mother and try for a boy, or you leave it to me."

"Cecilia, that isn't fair," her mother said. "You know we tried for other children, alas unsuccessfully."

Her father's face mottled in anger and for a moment Cecilia wondered if she'd pushed him too far with her words.

"How dare you, child. How dare you speak to us in such a way! I'm the head of this household, and under no circumstances shall you address me or your mother with so little regard or forethought."

Cecilia took a calming breath. How dare she? How dare they try and make her marry a man that made her skin crawl. "I may be your daughter, I may be female and looked upon as a lesser person in our Society, but I know I'm smarter than Mr. White and more than capable of keeping the men who work under you in control, motivated and in employment under my authority. You do not need to give it away to Mr. White simply because he's a man. You know, deep down what I'm saying is true, you simply have to trust me enough, love me enough to see that I'm worthy."

"You are worthy dear, never think that we believe anything other than that," her mother said, wringing her hands.

Her father shook his head, a deep frown line between his brows. "A woman would not be suitable, and it would only be a matter of time before people stopped seeking our services. I cannot risk the family's livelihood, a company I've taken twenty years to build up, to lose it simply to make my daughter happy. No," he said, standing and pouring himself a tumbler of brandy. "You shall marry Mr.

White and inherit the firm through him. It is more proper and suitable."

"Are you saying you're going to force me to marry him?" The horror of such a thought made her reach out and clasp the wall for support. To imagine Mr. White touching her again, not just kissing her, but sleeping next to her in bed, laying with her over and over. Her stomach recoiled, and she covered her mouth fearing she'd vomit.

Her mother came over and took her hand. "Mr. White isn't so bad, my dear. He's from a respectable family and is not unkind. You could do worse."

"While I do not want to force your hand, my dear, I will if you keep fighting me on this. I'll give you this season to become accustomed to Mr. White and his ways. Get to know him a little better. He isn't as bad as you may think, Cecilia."

He was worse. Cecilia looked out the window and watched as a coal cart rumbled by. She would ruin herself before she allowed herself to be married to such a prig. A slimy one at that.

She walked from the room and didn't reply. There was nothing left to say. Her parents' mind seemed made up and unless she found someone more suitable than Mr. White, better connected and willing to take on her father's firm, she would end up married to the man.

She paused at the bottom of the stairs. How could she bear such a life? She could not. She would not.

"Miss Smith, a letter from the Duchess of Athelby for you."

Cecilia took the parchment and broke the ducal seal. Scanning the letter quickly it stated that she was invited to a masquerade ball to be held at their good friends London estate, his lordship Hamish Doherty, Earl Leighton. The letter also said she could bring a guest.

She would take Katherine with her. She'd love to attend such a high Society event, and it would be one night that her future with Mr. White would be out of her mind. She had the season to convince her father. Otherwise, she would have to take matters and her life into her own hands and walk away from the family. She would not marry simply to ensure her father's company remained in their family. Such a bargain was neither fair nor right. She could become a teacher at one of the schools she'd opened. They raised their own funds, and other wealthy benefactors, such as the Duchess of Athelby might be willing to donate more to substitute the loss of her father's patronage, which she'd no doubt lose.

Even living on limited means as such a change in circumstance would ensue, was better than marrying a man she did not love. She would do anything but that.

A week passed, and finally, it was the night of the ball. The masquerade was a crush. The array of gowns, jewels, laughter and candlelight made the room seem like a glittering dream and Cecilia, and Katherine stood at the doors as the Duke and Duchess of Athelby walked ahead of them into the throng.

"Oh my, Cecilia. What a magnificent spectacle!"

Cecilia smiled and entwined her arm with Katherine's, pulling her forward. "It is truly a sight and one we shall never see again most likely. Promise me one thing tonight, my dear."

"Anything," Katherine said, her attention snapping from one costume to another.

There were many. The guests had outdone themselves with an array of characters present, jokers, pirates, mythical creatures and those who were less risqué, simply chose evening attire, silk gowns adorned with masks that sparked with jewels or feathers.

"That we forget where we're from, we take the opportunity to have fun, dance and laugh and forget all else."

"That sounds heavenly," Katherine said, smiling when a gentleman bowed before her in a flourishing, very much over the top manner, and asked her to dance. The man's costume was almost entirely black, foreboding even, and his mask covered his face entirely giving him an air of mystery.

Cecilia watched them disappear into the throng of dancers already on the ballroom floor and continued behind the duke and duchess.

They came to stand at the end of the long room beside the terrace doors which were open. Many of the guests were taking the opportunity to step out to take the air. The gardens were well lit, and outside looked just as pretty as the interior of the house.

Cecilia checked her attire. This evening she'd worn a white satin short sleeved gown with a green cape fastened on one of her shoulders that folded over her front, almost concealing her waist, but not quite. It was pinned to her hip by a pretty diamond paste broach her mother had loaned her for the evening. A single green plume was incorporated into her hair, and a plain silver mask concealing her eyes completed the outfit.

"Lord Leighton has gone to a lot of trouble for this ball. Does he hold it yearly?"

"He does," the duchess said, taking the glass of champagne her husband passed to her, before giving it to Cecilia. "I remember last year when I attended, my husband who wasn't my husband at the time didn't approve."

The duke looked down his nose at Darcy before he grinned. "I approve now, my dear."

Cecilia looked away as it seemed a private, husband and wife conversation was happening between the pair and she didn't want to intrude.

"I believe Lord Aaron will be here this evening."

"As to that, my dear." The duke scanned the crowd, frowning a little. "Hunter may be late. I believe he's bringing a guest."

"Really," the duchess said, casting a glance in Cecilia's direction. "Who?"

Cecilia picked out Lord Aaron well before the duke said anything else, and she watched as his lordship made his way over to them. Tonight Lord Aaron seemed bedraggled, his hair hardly tamed and the stubble growth of his beard barely covered by the mask that he wore. The woman holding his arm oozed breeding and rank, and she looked stunning in her red empire style gown with gold embroidered flowers about its hem.

Cecilia turned her attention back to the dancers and tried to ignore the ringing in her ears. The room spun, and distantly she heard the duke of Athelby curse. Unable to stop herself, her attention snapped back to the pair coming toward them while she tried not to die of humiliation. Did he make sport of kissing many women in carriages and then attend balls with new lovers? Not that he owed her anything. He'd surely not promised her courtship, or that their kiss was the beginning of an understanding, but really, what was he about. As it stood, he certainly looked like the ass he'd painted himself the first day she'd met him.

Lord Aaron bowed before them, hardly glancing in her direction when he bade her a good evening.

The duchess smiled at the woman and gestured her

toward Cecilia. "Miss Smith, may I introduce you to Lady Henrietta Morton, recently from Bath if memory serves me correctly."

Lady Morton curtsied. The woman's eyes were glassy and a little bloodshot, similar to Lord Aaron's. "Your grace, it's lovely to be back in town. Bath, as you understand, is only very small, and when Lord Aaron begged me to come to town, well, how could I refuse him?"

How indeed... "You live in Bath most of the time, your ladyship?" Cecilia asked, not wanting to seem rude and uninterested in Lord Aaron's partner. She took a calming breath and smiled tentatively even though her hands shook in her silk gloves. What a fool she'd been. A silly little game to his lordship and now his new little game was smirking at her in return.

"I'm sorry, who are you?" Lady Morton asked, inspecting her as if she were a bug.

Cecilia fought not to fidget. "I'm Miss Cecilia Smith, your ladyship." Cecilia took a glass of ratafia from a passing footman, anything to help keep her hands from giving her unease away.

"Are you related to the Smiths of Hampshire? They reside at Woodrest Abbey."

"Ah, no," Cecilia said, taking a sip of her drink. "My father's a barrister and runs J Smith and Sons law firm in Cheapside."

Her ladyship laughed, and the duchess glared at the woman, but Lady Morton took no heed of the silent warning from her better, merely continued to chuckle. "And you're here, why? I didn't think these events allowed people of your ilk to attend."

Cecilia bobbed a small curtsy. "The same could be said of you, Lady Morton for you have no manners and therefore no class. Please excuse me," she said, heading toward the retirement room, hating the fact her ladyship's cutting remarks had gotten the better of her. She needed to get away from the woman before she said anything else as rude as what her ladyship said.

Entering the foyer, she followed a small group of women who were talking and walking toward their mutual destination. How dare Lady Morton speak to her in such a way and how dare Lord Aaron allow it. She might be of a lower class, but she was friends with a duchess, that at least should afford her some meagre amount of respect.

An arm came about her waist and pulled her into a small sitting room opposite the retirement room that she was about to enter. Before she turned, Cecilia knew who was behind her, and she masked her features before facing Lord Aaron. He had played his cards and shown their value, and she would not be fooled again.

"What are you doing here? The duchess never informed me that she was inviting you this evening."

Cecilia raised her brows, nonplussed. "And she has to inform you of everything she does? I think not. Excuse me," she said, making for the door.

He pulled her back, and she caught the stench of whisky on his breath. "Already in your cups, my lord. How very original of you."

Lord Aaron swallowed, running a hand over his face and pulling off his mask. "I was going to call on you."

She narrowed her eyes, staunchly ignoring the butterflies taking flight in her stomach. "And why would you do that? We are not friends nor do we circulate in the same Society. I'm only here by invitation by the duchess. And I can promise you, after tonight, I will not be attending another ball near any of you people." She would exclude the duchess of course from this, but everyone else could go hang.

"Lady Morton is an old friend of my family, a woman who's been brought down financially by her late husband. Being the younger son of a penniless duke, they were never flush with cash. She merely asked me for assistance in helping her re-establish herself in London. There is nothing romantically happening between us if your prickly attitude toward me has any explanation."

She sucked in a very audible breath. "Excuse me, Lord Aaron I am not prickly in any way. And if I was rude about your friend, it was merely because she was very impolite. I'll not be talked down to from anyone, least of all a woman who smells as strongly of liquor as you do."

A muscle on his jaw clenched. "May I remind you that your continual reminders and sly remarks about my intake of alcohol are not acceptable. Not by anyone."

She shrugged. "I care not what is or isn't acceptable. You, Lord Aaron, are always foxed, slurring your words, and bringing women of questionable morals to balls. Do you not see how unacceptable that is? If your friends will not try and help you see a better way forward than being in your cups all the time, caring for nothing but folly and how you can spend your precious money on unimportant things, then I shall. There is nothing lost if we are not friends."

His lordship stepped in front of her when she went to make another escape. What was the man's problem! She glared up at him. "Move out of my way."

"Nothing lost? Do you mean that?"

"You continue to prove my point. No man who was not drunk would ever ask a woman so forward a question. You are practically asking if I like you, and you should not and would not if you weren't so drunk."

"I'm not that drunk," he said, swaying a little toward her.

Cecilia crossed her arms. His gaze veered to her bosom, slightly pushed up because of her stance, so she dropped her arms at her side.

"I think there would be a great opportunity lost if you walked out of my life."

"You made me feel like a fool. I kissed you and then you arrive at a ball with another woman. I know you've made no promises to me, and I have no expectations, but you should at least, as a gentleman, act with some sensitivity. Now if you'll excuse me, Lord Aaron, I wish to leave."

❧

HUNTER SWALLOWED the panic that coursed through him at Cecilia's words. He'd not thought she would be at Lord Leighton's masked ball. He'd only brought Lady Morton this evening to reintroduce her to a Society she'd been absent from for some years. No harm in that.

Stupid mistake seeing Miss Smith was in attendance, and it made him look like he had women at his beck and call. Brought them to balls and parties without thought to women, or to at least one woman whom he'd kissed with abandon only last week.

"You may be right, I may drink more than I ought, but know this. There is nothing between Lady Morton and myself. I will admit to having relations with her during her marriage, which is not my proudest moment I grant you, but I have not, and I am not looking to renew those relations anytime soon."

Hunter clasped her chin and brought her crystal blue eyes back to look at him. Hell, she was pretty, with a mouth that begged to be kissed, and damn it, he wanted to kiss her again. Had thought of little else since last week.

"If you must know the truth, I think of you. Of your

opinionated self, of your intelligent conversations and witty repertoire. Of your beauty both in and out. Your charitable personality that leaves me to shame. You are the only woman who's not throwing themselves at my feet, and it is literally driving me to distraction."

She did look at him then, her perfectly straight teeth clasping her bottom lip and driving him even more obsessed with her person.

"I think about you all the time. I think about kissing you all the time," he murmured.

"You wish to kiss me again, Lord Aaron?"

He nodded before caution could halt his reply. "Yes, I do," he said, not willing to hide anymore his feelings toward the woman before him. Not wanting to, if he were honest. She would be the perfect mistress, keep him interested and never bored. Blast it all, he wanted to taste her again if she'd allow.

"If you ever wish to kiss me again, my lord the price you need to pay is the liquor you're so fond of. Do not touch a drink at any event up until you see me again, and I shall grant you such a boon."

His gut clenched at the thought of not having brandy in front of his fire at home, or a lovely, well-aged whisky at events such as this. "Am I allowed wine?"

"No, tea and coffee are acceptable, along with fruit punch, so long as it's alcohol-free. And if you are then, my lord, still interested in kissing a woman half your rank, a bluestocking well on the shelf, sober of course, then I shall allow you to kiss me," she said, with a stubborn lift of her chin.

"You think I only want you because I'm in my cups? Which by the way, I'd like to point out I'm not that drunk." He hated that she was thinking such things. It couldn't be more from the truth. There had been many times he'd thought of her, wanted her and had not taken one ounce of drink.

"I do think that."

He frowned. "Well don't, because when I win this war, and I'm standing before you sober, you will experience and see just how much I want you for you, not because of any liquid courage." And then he would ask her to consider being his mistress, allow him to pamper and care for her in a mutually satisfying manner.

His life up to the point when he'd met her was filled with nothing but self-gratification. Cecilia was a pure soul, made him want to be a better man. Due to her rank, he could never look at her as anything other than a lover, but that didn't mean he couldn't make her life sweeter, make his own life worth more than how it currently stood. With such a lifestyle she could continue her charity work and never have to worry about marrying anyone to keep a roof over the children's head that she cared for.

She gazed up at him, innocent and yet there was a strength, and intelligence that lurked in her cerulean orbs and he wanted that for himself. He wanted her in his life. Hunter straightened his back and bowed. "I will ensure you're invited to the next event the duke and duchess attend, and there, Miss Smith, you shall lose this wager."

She reached up and clasped his jaw, and he stilled at the feel of her touch. At some point, she'd removed her gloves, and her soft hand was warm and comforting, making his gut clench. "No, Lord Aaron, don't you see, I shall win either way and so too will you."

"Will you dance with me?"

CECILIA NODDED. "YES."

74

They made their way back to the ballroom to the orchestra playing a waltz. Cecilia spied Katherine dancing with another masked stranger, and the duke and duchess too were partaking in the risqué dance.

"Do you like to dance, Miss Smith?" the marquess asked, twirling her quickly and making her laugh.

"I do, although we do not go out as much as we used to during my debut. If it hasn't passed your notice, I'm quite on the shelf."

"You never wished to marry?" he asked her, watching her so closely that heat spread through her veins. Did he like what he saw? Did his questioning of her mean he wanted to get to know her better?

"I was courted, but I never found any gentleman whom I cared for enough to give myself to. And so I threw myself into charity work, found a new love, that of the children who rely on me. I'm not concerned if I never marry, no matter what my father may think. I'm quite content with my situation in life."

He shook his head at her words. "You're so confident in your direction. I fear I have little. I suppose I truly do look like a fop who does nothing with his life, other than spend it unwisely."

His hand tightened about her waist during a turn, and her heart thumped in her chest. She swallowed. "You do not have to live in such a way. You're a powerful lord, think of all the wonderful things you could do if only you wished to."

"Give to charity, you mean? Not build my gentleman's club," he asked grinning.

She chuckled. "Not just that, you could pursue other venues to help others, like enter the house of Lords and seek change for the poor. Stop children from having to work and instead send them to school. Better housing for the poor, better water supply, drainage, and heating for their homes."

He shook his head. "I'm in awe of you, Miss Smith. I do believe you're born before your time. Never have I ever met someone with such determined, good opinions. A steadfastness to try and make others' lives better. You shame me."

"No," she said, not wanting him to think in such a way. "I'm far from perfect, like you I have my flaws. I'm opinionated and judgemental, as you've seen. Not everyone has the stomach for the work I do, and I should be more understanding of that, not condone and condemn."

"Sometimes, as with me, it's appropriate, but I know, with your help I can change, possibly make changes in my life and others."

Cecilia smiled, having not thought she'd ever hear his lordship state such. He'd been so impossibly blind to others that she'd placed him in the box of no hope. "I know you can."

CHAPTER 8

The following week Cecilia sat in her father's library, crafting letters to his clients on their updates and progress as per her father's notes. It was an occupation she enjoyed and since her hand was more legible than her father's it was something he allowed her to do for him.

A loud, knock sounded at the door, and Cecilia placed her quill down as the voice, speaking quickly to their butler was familiar. The library door swung wide, and the Duchess of Athelby strolled into the room, her usually serene countenance, reddened by exertion and marred by worry.

Cecilia stood. "Your grace, is everything well?"

The duchess came to stand before the desk, shaking her head. "You must come with me. The Marquess of Aaron is in a terrible state. Now, before you say anything, hear me out."

The duchess paused, and Cecilia nodded her approval.

"He mentioned to the duke that you'd made a wager with him, one that he has taken very seriously over the last seven days. So much so, that he's become very unwell."

A warmth flowed through her veins that the marquess had gone through with his promise. Did it mean he cared for her, maybe saw her as someone to spend the rest of his life with, have a family of their own? Is he someone she would want to spend the rest of her life with? Cecilia gestured for the duchess to sit and took a seat herself, dismissing the thought. Never had the marquess stated anything of the kind, other than wanting to kiss her he'd made no promises to her. She shouldn't get ahead of herself. "May I speak, your grace? Plainly, if you will allow."

"Of course, but this is not all I have to tell you."

"I think I know what the rest of your words will be, but may I tell you what I know?"

The duchess nodded, wringing her hands in her lap. "Of course."

"Working in the charities that I do, we see similarities with people who suffer from different afflictions. I don't know if you're aware, but I fear the Marquess of Aaron cannot control himself when it comes to wine or whisky, drinks of that nature. To brutally say it, he is a drunk, your grace. A very well spoken and dressed one at that, but even so, he has barrel fever. Our wager was for him to cease drinking, and he is now having repercussions due to his choice. It is not pleasant, and it will take time, but he will get through this."

The Duchess stared at her a moment before she said, "While I admit to being aware somewhat of this affliction, what is happening to him now is not at all good. He's very unwell, and he's asking for you. Will not allow anyone else to see him. Cameron is worried sick, and even though what I'm asking you to do is beyond proper, will you come with me. Help me, help him."

Cecilia stood, not needing to be asked twice. The thought of Hunter suffering made her stomach recoil. "Of course, I'll help. Let me pack a small valise. When I go to visit the orphanage in the country, I always sleep over. I'll leave a message for papa stating that is where I've gone. He'll not assume I've gone to the marquess's home instead."

The duchess clasped her hand. "You're very good, and we will keep your name and your visitation to the marquess's home secret, I promise you that. We'll not allow anyone to know that you were there."

***

IT WASN'T long before the duchess' unmarked carriage pulled into the mews at the back of the marquess's home on Berkeley Square. A stable hand came out and helped them down, before going through the back garden to ensure they weren't seen arriving and headed indoors.

The home was not what Cecilia had expected. For some reason, she'd assumed the house would be dark, mysterious just like its owner, but instead, it was brightly lit, wax candles burning in every room and hallway. There were well-kept carpet rugs and highly polished floorboards. The staircase that sat centre in the entrance hall too was well lit, and from the base of the stairs, Cecilia could see that the first-floor landing housed many portraits, possibly of past family members.

"Shall we go up?" the duchess asked, stepping toward the stairs.

"Of course. I'll follow you." They went upstairs, and the duke met them on the landing.

"He still will not allow me to enter." The duke bowed.

"Good afternoon, Miss Smith. I do apologize for our intrusion into your day, but we would not have done so had we not thought it the most important."

Cecilia curtsied. "Do not tax yourself, your grace. It was my silly bet with the marquess which has brought on his current symptoms, it is only right that I try and alleviate them in some way."

"You're too kind," the duchess said. "Hunter's room is the third door on the left. We shall go downstairs and order some tea. Please have a servant fetch us if there is anything we can do to help. There is one outside his door at all times. Unfortunately, it is not us the marquess was asking for."

"I shall," Cecilia said, making her way to the room and placing her bag beside the door. She stood there without making a sound while she watched the duke and duchess head downstairs. Taking a deep breath, she knocked hard twice.

"Lord Aaron, will you let me in? It's Miss Smith."

No sound came from the room, and just before she was about to knock again, the lock turned, and the door swung wide. He was worse than Cecilia had imagined, and without saying a word, she entered the room, leaving the door ajar just the slightest.

Taking his lordship's hand, she walked him over to the fire, which was nothing but coals and sat him down. Turning to the hearth, she added some more coal, then wood, and blew on the embers that still glowed red, but no longer formed any heat. She concentrated on her task, creating a draft with the fire, and thankfully a few spots of the wood took light, and the fire started to burn.

"You are the most accomplished woman I know. You can even create fire."

She laughed, standing and taking a seat across from him. "Growing up we didn't have a lot of servants, and even though we are able to afford them now, it was not always the case. And so yes, I learned how to do many things. I can wash clothes, cook food, dust and clean, even make fires. Not what your Society would call accomplished, but I think they're excellent life skills that everyone should have."

He stared at her, his eyes glassy, and dark-ringed with tiredness. His hair was matted and looked in need of a good wash. He was a right state, and she frowned, guilt pricking her soul. "You know why I'm here don't you, my lord?"

The marquess cringed, turning his attention to the fire. "Call me Hunter, please. You're seeing me at my worst, I do not deserve the name of a gentleman in this condition."

"I shall call you Hunter, but you are worthy of the title, my lord. Your condition does not make you who you are. It is simply a symptom of what you've been doing to yourself."

If broken had a face, the marquess would be a portrait of it. "I feel like horse dung, and I do beg your pardon on the use of such a word, but I never felt so ill in my life. But even so, my desire to be worthy of your kiss overrides my misery."

Cecilia's heart did a little flip, and she fought not to go to him, to wrap him in her arms and give him what he wanted. What she wanted. But not yet, first they had to vanquish this inner demon he fought against and beat it. The pain she read in his eyes made her question her decision, not that to help, but to keep at a distance. Maybe she would be a better addiction for him than the one he now fought.

Against her better judgement, she kneeled at his feet. Clasping his stubble roughened cheeks she pulled him toward her, kissing him gently on the mouth. The feel of him so close, the touch of his breath against her lips left her longing for more. Even in his state, both physically and mentally, she wanted to kiss him. Allow him to lose himself in her, anything but allow the need for more of what he'd been imbibing himself in for however many years he'd been drinking.

"You are worthy, never think otherwise," she said softly.

Even as uneducated in the art of love that she was, she was able to distinguish the burning desire he had for her when she saw it. And she saw it now, in the depths of his eyes, a yearning to be free, to forget what ailed him and lose himself in her.

Cecilia kissed him again, leaning up and taking his mouth in much the same way as he'd kissed her in the carriage. Unhindered, without restraint and with a need that pulled at her own wants and desires she'd long buried.

Hunter as he now wanted her to call him roused all her buried wants, her dreams of a life with a man. Not just any man, like the one her father wished her to marry, but a man who excited her, stimulated her mind and soul, vexed and maddened in all the most wonderful ways.

A life with Lord Aaron…

"I've longed for you. You make me forget who I've been, and see what I can become." His voice, roughened and deep sent her pulse to skip a beat. She fought not to kiss him again until they were both lost in their own world. "Let me love you. Let me have you."

Cecilia leaned back and captured his gaze. "I will stay with you, help you as best as I know how, but I cannot allow you the liberties that you ask. But I will give you as much as I can."

"Your soul is so pure. Mine is as dark as the devil himself."

She caressed his stubble roughened cheek. "Then it is lucky that I do not have idle hands, for there is no place in this room for the devil's work and you will be well again. I promise you that."

CHAPTER 9

By late that evening Lord Aaron was wrenching about in his bed, his skin clammy and dripping with sweat. His lordship constantly begged for a dram of whisky, anything, anyone to help him. Cecilia ordered the butler to pour all the remaining alcohol in the home down the drain, and she also ordered the cook to hide any beverages of the kind that she used in her cooking. Nothing was to remain in the house that his lordship could drink if any one of them turned their back on him for even a moment.

Cecilia sat beside his bed, holding his hand. "Please, Lia, just a little drink," he said, making the nickname he'd bestowed on her sound endearing, even if he only seemed to have used it in the last few hours. It was the name her mother had called her as a child, and she adored it, even more, coming from the lips of Lord Aaron.

She shouldn't, of course, he was so far above her in station, had demons that even she didn't know if they could remove, not to mention to marry such a man could limit her charities or at least the amount she was involved in them. He may have previously stated he wished to change, to help others, but what if that lifestyle bored him. What if he grew weary of her.

Cecilia was terrible at needlework or idly walking in parks merely to be seen, she had always felt out of place in such situations. Not to mention, her father relied upon her too, to help out with his cases and do his bookwork. Not that Mr. White thought she was useful, but Cecilia had always harboured the idea that if she could prove to her father she was capable, he would allow her to inherit.

Would the marquess in time expect her to be a pretty ornament on his arm, behave and hold her tongue. The life of one of the upper ten-thousand was not for her, no matter how much his lordship beckoned her soul to try. The risk was great, and she wasn't sure she was capable of such a gamble.

But she would assist him like she helped so many people in need. Help him regain who he once was so he may marry wisely and hopefully with love and affection. Make more of his life than the silly folly he'd partaken in to date.

"I cannot give you what you want, Hunter." She bathed his forehead with a damp cloth and tried to soothe him with talk of her charities, of idle gossip, anything to take his mind off what his body craved. The hours ticked by and as dawn broke the night sky into a golden haze, Lord Aaron was worse.

She stood beside the duke, biting her bottom lip as she thought of how to keep his lordship safe, from himself and others. "We need to tie him to the bed. He's too large to control, and if he took flight, it would take a lot of us to overpower him. His need for alcohol will make his strength double."

"How do you know all this, Miss Smith?" the duke asked, looking down at her.

She frowned, staring at the marquess who lay crunched up on the bed, clutching at his stomach. "As you know, I work and run charities for children mostly, but I do have a small charity that I run for the parents of the children I help. These parents have never had a good life, never had opportunities and at every turn, seemed to be kicked and trodden on by life and those who should be there to guide and help them make the right choices. A lot of these parents have drinking problems or other medicinal addictions. The troubles Lord Aaron now faces means it'll be a month before he's feeling himself again. But he'll never be truly free. This fight will be a life-long one I'm afraid."

"God help him. And God bless you for doing such charity. I know my duchess speaks quite highly of you, and now I know why."

Cecilia nodded, but the fear and concern she had for the marquess did diminish the kernel of pride that the duke awoke in her. He was so very ill, perhaps more addicted than she had imagined. "The duchess has been a pillar of strength and friendship for me these past twelve months. I cannot tell you how much I appreciate her help. We need more of it if we're to change the boroughs of London and their outcomes for those less fortunate."

"I'm sure you will always have it."

The marquess yelled out, groaning and Cecilia walked to his tall chest of drawers and rummaged through his clothing until she found what she was looking for. "Take these cravats and tie his arms to the bedhead. The marquess will have to be contained for the next few days possibly."

The staff who stood in the room looked horrified by her words, but with a nod from the duke, they did as she asked. Seeing the marquess in his current state left a hollow void in her chest. How she loathed that he fought such demons, had well and truly lost against them, but no more. She would help him through this, she and his friends would not let him fail this test.

The day wore on, and the duchess came to sit with her for a few hours, gave Cecilia time to bathe and allow Hunter's manservant to wash his master. Evening approached, and Cecilia stood at the marquess's windows that overlooked his back garden and stared at the silver light from the moon that bathed the garden.

"Cecilia, come sit with me."

She turned to see the marquess staring at her from under hooded lids, eyes that were slowly clearing and becoming clearer as the alcohol left his body. Walking over to him, she sat on the edge of the bed, taking the opportunity to bathe his forehead and face. He was so very handsome, even in his state and dishevelment she had to admit that she liked him, was attracted to him from the very first moment she'd met him. She wiped the cloth down his neck to the vee of his shirt.

Heat prickled her skin as her imagination ran away from her. What was she doing thinking about what lay under his shirt with his lordship as sick as he was?

"I'm going to be sick, Cecilia. Please, untie me and fetch me the bowl. Quickly," he said.

She did as he asked, and only just managed to get the bowl over to the bed before he cast up his accounts. He heaved, over and over before flopping back onto the bed, spent.

Cecilia rang for a servant, ordering tea and ginger biscuits if the cook had any. She then went about removing Hunter's shirt, wiping his clammy body down, all the while trying not to blush or gawk at the toned muscles that had a fine dusting of hair. Over the next few days, his lordship's progress ebbed and flowed in an array of stages. Anger, contrite, begging to railing at them all. Having been away from home for a few days, she returned to Cheapside, only to find her father waiting for her in his library.

"I wish to speak with you, Cecilia. Now."

His tone didn't bode well, and a small stab of concern pierced her gut. She entered the room, features masked, only to find Mr. White seated before her father, his slimy features smirking in her direction.

"Good morning, father. Mr., White."

"You're back from your orphanage in Hampshire I see."

She did as he bade and clasped her hands in her lap. "As you see. My work there took a few days longer than I expected, and later today I'm to attend a charity meeting at Old Bell Tavern."

Her father stared at her with indifference and the concern she had before doubled. Why was he so out of sorts? And why was Mr. White here? Her father knew she hated the man, especially after he took liberties in the carriage that were not returned. The vile piece of flesh had no shame and her father either did not believe her or did not care.

Cecilia pushed down the hurt that thought conjured, and steeled herself for what she feared was to come.

"I had some time the last two days, and so I took the opportunity to visit you in Hampshire, but you can imagine my surprise when I arrived at your country school and orphanage only to hear the headmistress tell me she had not seen or heard from you in relation to your supposed visit. I returned home but found you were not here or at any of the London orphanages and schools you run. So," her father said, steepling his hands beneath his chin, the frown line between his eyes as deep as the Thames river. "Where were you, Cecilia?"

She swallowed and refused to look at the smirking Mr. White who for the first time in his life had no opinion it would seem on her disappearance. "A father of one of the children was in need of help. I along with the people who assist me often with these types of troubles, helped me nurse him, and he's now recovering at home."

"Really, then please do explain why Mr. White saw you enter Lord Aaron's home. A place you have been ensconced the past few days?"

Cecilia did look at the little vermin then. How she loathed the man, his greed and uncharitable nature. "You followed me? How dare you?"

He merely chuckled before the slamming of her father's fist on the table broke her fury directed at the bastard.

"How dare Mr. White? How dare you, Cecilia. Are you mad, child? To be entering an unmarried gentleman's home in the dead of night? What were you doing there? No, please, don't answer that," he said standing and rounding the table toward her. He pulled her to stand, and for the first time in her life he manhandled her, squeezing her arms. "How dare you place your reputation in jeopardy in such a way. I ought to throw you out of my home."

Cecilia wrenched free and took a step away from her father. Never had she seen him so angry before. His voice was calm, yet there was a steel tone of loathing she'd never heard before and panic lodged in her throat that maybe she'd overstepped his bounds.

"I apologize for helping Lord Aaron, but it was at the behest of the duke and duchess of Athelby. They were there the entire time, you may ask them yourself. And if you're worried that Lord Aaron abused me in some way you're mistaken. We are simply trying to get him better."

"Well, I shall ask the duke and duchess what they think

they're doing taking my unmarried, maiden daughter into the home of a renowned rake. I shall ask them to explain their high and mighty decision to put your reputation in jeopardy. You, Cecilia, shall heed this warning, and you shall do as I say from this moment on."

Her gaze flicked to Mr. White who again looked too pleased for himself by far. "What do you mean by that? And as for my reputation, I can assure you it is quite sound and not in any jeopardy unless this information is leaked to Society and what I've been doing the last few days becomes public knowledge."

Her father stiffened. "Are you insinuating that Mr. White would go to the press with such rumours?"

"If it made it impossible for you to refuse his designs of me becoming his wife, then yes, I think him capable of such underhanded ways."

Mr. White feigned shock, clasping his chest for added dramatics. "I would never do such a thing, Mr. Smith. I assure you."

Cecilia scoffed. "You are no gentleman, Sir. No man of any moral value assaults women in carriages. And if you think I'm going to marry this swine because I have helped Lord Aaron you're sadly mistaken. I shall walk away from my life here with you if you try and force my hand and make me marry Mr. White."

Her father's face mottled in anger. "You have no choice but to marry Mr. White as without doing so I shall stop all funding toward the charities you're so very fond of. It is about time that you settled, had children that will inherit the firm. Mr. White is willing to take your hand, even if this latest news becomes public knowledge and your repu-tation is ruined. He is smart, from a respectable family and loves you. You will obey, Cecilia. That is my final word."

Cecilia stormed from the room, slamming the door

closed behind her. Tears blurred her vision as she climbed the stairs. How dare either of them speak and demand such things of her? She would not do it, she could not give herself to such a man.

She made it to her room and snipping the lock went to stand at the window. Hundreds of children relied on her. Many, many families needed her to give them a chance, to keep the orphanages and schools going so their children might have some future. She had no doubt her father would be as vindictive as he threatened and take away the funds, therefore unless she had a large investor who was willing to take the expense on, there was nothing she could do. The Duchess of Athelby already donated a significant amount, she couldn't ask for more, it wouldn't be fair.

Would it?

Cecilia worked her bottom lip, before sitting at her desk and pulling out a piece of parchment. She could never marry a man she did not love so she would have to beg the duchess for help. Her pride would need to take a seat so she could secure her other greatest love, the children. That was all that mattered now.

CHAPTER 10

Hunter squinted as the bright sunlight streamed into his room. He stared at the blue sky beyond and did a mental check of how he felt. *Good*. Better than he'd felt for a long time. Weeks in fact and he knew who he had to thank for such nursing. The same woman who sat beside the fire, mending a button on one of his shirts if he weren't mistaken.

The image was so reminiscent of a married, family life that he smiled. He liked having her here, talking to him, calming him, being in his room as if it was a common and ordinary thing for her to do.

Which it was not.

Even he knew in his state of delirium that Miss Smith, Lia as he'd come to call her, should not be here, chaperoned by the Duke and Duchess of Athelby or not.

"Lia, can you ring for tea, please. I'm in need of sustenance."

She looked up, her bright blue eyes twisting an emotion in his chest he didn't want to think about at the moment, although when better, he would have to admit for what he'd come to feel toward her. Miss Smith was quite literally the woman who saved his life.

He adored her.

"How are you feeling this morning," she said, coming over and sitting on his bed as if it were the most normal thing to do. They were on dangerous ground, Lia and him. Should she have sat on his bed when he was in his cups, there was no doubt he would've leaned forward and kissed those, perfectly rosy lips and try and seduce her.

"For the first time in as long as I can remember I feel clear headed." His stomach rumbled and Cecilia chuckled. "And I'm hungry by the sounds of that," he said, smiling.

"I'll have breakfast brought up to you as soon as they arrive with your tea." She rose from the bed and sat in the chair beside it, seemingly rethinking her location. "I thought we'd go outside for a little while today. You've been indoors for almost a month, and it would do you good to have fresh air and a little sun."

The idea, as menial and boring as it sounded lifted his spirits. It would be delightful to be out of this room, as long as he had Cecilia's company. "You will join me?"

"I will. I'm here until lunch, and then the duchess and duke will take over for me. We have a little schedule going, you see." She smiled, a sincere gesture he didn't see too often in the *ton*. Hunter studied her, she was a marvellous girl, and she would make a perfect mistress. He would lavish her with gifts and freedom she'd never known, so long as she shared his bed, and only his bed.

THREE WEEKS later Hunter was well enough to attend his first evening out about town. The duke and duchess sat across from him in the landau. They hadn't said the words, but Hunter understood why they were with him. To watch and ensure he did not lapse into the life of drunkenness and folly that he'd partaken in before.

Miss Smith sat beside him, her pensive gaze staring out at the busy streets beyond. Over the last week, she'd been distant, pulling away from him whenever she came to keep him company and ensure again he didn't seek out his whisky.

Although the staff had poured out every ounce they found, Hunter had his own little bottle hidden in his room, and yet he'd not sought it out. It was almost a test against himself, a wager to see if he had the willpower not to touch it.

Not that it hadn't been hard ignoring it, it was torture. He longed to feel the burn of the golden liquid sliding down his throat, leaving him warm and comforted. Losing the ability to handle his drink, not being able to have such repast in the future was a longing he fought every day to ignore. If it weren't for his friends, Lia included, he would not have made it as far as he had.

The light headed beauty beside him met his gaze as if she was privy to his thoughts. He would kiss her tonight, sneak her away and do what he'd wanted to for weeks.

The carriage rolled to a stop before Sir Colten's London home, and they waited for a footman to become available to open their door. Once inside, they greeted their hosts and made their way through the throng of guests.

Some cast odd glances at the appearance of Miss Smith, a woman not of their sphere, who in some of their eyes should not be attending. But with the Duke and Duchess of Athelby supporting her, they dare not speak a word about it.

Cecilia shone like a diamond in a sea of paste, and the

temptation to dance with her grew. Hunter looked over to where the musicians sat, playing music that was congenial for conversation. Other guests gathered on the floor, and it wouldn't be long before the dancing began.

They stopped before one of three fireplaces in the room, and Hunter held out his hand to Miss Smith. "Will you dance with me?"

She took his hand, nodding slightly. "Thank you, yes."

The strains of a waltz started to play, and Hunter could've dropped to his knees in thankfulness. The perfect dance for seduction, for talking intimately.

"You're very beautiful this evening, Lia," he said, drinking in every nuance of her right down to the little freckle that sat above her lip.

"You're very handsome."

She blushed, and he laughed, pulling her a little closer than he ought.

"You also smell divine. What is that scent?"

"Jasmine." She tipped her head to the side, eyeing him. "You're flirting with me, Lord Aaron."

"Can I not flirt with the prettiest woman in attendance?" The slide of her silk gown against his palm sent desire coiling through him. He wanted her, all of her, to be his, now and forever. He would not survive without her he was sure.

"And now that I'm better and being watched day and night by my valet due to the duke's strict instructions, you'll not be able to visit me anymore. Come up to my room and nurse me back to health," he said wiggling his eyebrows.

Cecilia laughed. It was about time she did so, she'd been reserved and troubled, a constant frown had formed between her eyes whenever she didn't think anyone was watching, but he was. "Is everything well, Lia. You seem unsettled about something."

She bit her bottom lip, and he pulled her close as they manoeuvred a turn. "Tell me what it is. I want to help you if I can, just as you helped me."

❦

CECILIA FOUGHT to keep her attention on the guests that lined the dance floor and not at Lord Aaron, Hunter as he wished to be called. If she looked at him, she would be lost. She sighed. Who was she kidding, she was already lost. "My father found out about me helping you. He knows I was in your bedroom, unchaperoned at times. He does not know what ailed you, but he's aware only that you had an illness that the Duke and Duchess of Athelby asked me to help with."

"Why has he not called on me and demanded that I ask for your hand?"

"What?" Cecilia lowered her tone and met the marquess's gaze. "Because he doesn't want me to marry you."

"What! What do you mean he doesn't want me to marry you? I'm a marquess, a rich lord, I could give you everything and more. Why has he not come to me, that is the most preposterous notion I've ever heard."

Cecilia couldn't help but chuckle at Hunter's self-praise, and she patted his shoulder to ease his tension. "There are two reasons, one that is my own doing I'm afraid."

"And what is that?"

"I've always been critical of those who are more fortunate than so many. As much as I have enjoyed the duke and duchess' company, and your own, especially now as you're more yourself, after your illness, this is not my world. I do not fit in here. I'm too rough about the edges, too willing to get down on my hands and knees and scrub floors if it's required. Too often I take sick children home and nurse them back to health. I could do none of those things as a Society wife. My father understands this about me, and does not think I would suit the life of a lord's wife."

"And the second reason?"

"Father will be announcing my betrothal to Mr. White Friday next. He has threatened to remove his patronage to my orphanages and schools I worked so hard to build. He has threatened to give the firm to Mr. White and leave me nothing if I do not do as I'm told, especially now that my reputation is sullied, or would be sullied if my visiting of you was to be made public knowledge."

"Like hell he did." A muscle ticked on Hunter's jaw, and looking about he pulled her from the dance and escorted her onto the terrace. Seeing an array of couples, he turned away from them all and started toward the stairs at one end that led to the gardens.

Nerves fluttered in Cecilia's stomach, and the strong, determined line of Hunter's jaw left her mouth dry. What was he thinking? What he was about to do was anyone's guess, but if she could wish for one thing, it would be to kiss him again. To take one last memory of him before she lowered herself, even more, out of his sphere and became a teacher at her schools. With the duchess having confirmed that she would become the charity's principal sponsor, it was safe no matter what her father decided.

He walked along the side of the house, and seeing a stone chair against the wall, pulled her down to sit. "I will not allow you to marry Mr. White. He is vile for one, and you do not care for him."

"I have no intention of marrying Mr. White. I have secured the safety of my charities for the years to come, but by doing so, by denying my father his wishes, I shall suffer the consequences."

"How do you mean you'll suffer the consequences," he asked, beseeching her to tell him the truth.

"When I tell my father that I no longer require his help with my schools, and when I tell him that I will not marry his heir, I have no doubt he will banish me. Maybe even throw me out. I'm to become a teacher, and have already prepared lodgings at Spitalfields orphanage."

He frowned, leaning away. "A teacher, a tutor, but that is beneath you, Cecilia. I'm sure you've not thought of all your options."

She sighed, having searched her mind for days trying to think of other options, but she was tired of it. Cecilia would by far prefer to be a tutor than have Mr. Smith as her husband. The only thing that tinged her choice with regret was that the marquess would never look to her as his wife. She would well and truly be beneath his gaze now. "It is done, my lord. And that is that."

Cecilia met his gaze hoping it was disappointment she read within his stormy blue orbs. "I will not deny that even with your troubles and that we did not start out as friends, I find you the most interesting, and vexing man I've ever met. A man that after one kiss left me questioning my own rules, my own opinions of what I wished for in life. But I'm happy with my choice, and although my forays into your Society will come to an end, I do not regret our time or our friendship. I hope I shall always have it."

He cupped her face, and as if in a trance Cecilia watched as Hunter closed the distance between them and kissed her. In relative darkness, she slid her arms around his neck and kissed him back, wanting to take this one moment and capture the memory forever.

Cecilia gasped when his tongue slid against hers, an

odd but enjoyable sensation that pooled heat at her core. Her breasts strained against her gown, and without knowing why, she pushed against him, his firm, warm body relieving a little of the need that coursed through her blood.

"You cannot kiss me like this Lia," he said, his lips feathering kisses down her throat, "and become a tutor, leave me alone in all this pomp and ceremony. We may be opposites, but in this we are equal."

She clasped his hair, a gasp escaped as his tongue ran against the top of her breasts where her gown began. "Just kiss me, Hunter, and let me forget everything else."

He did as she bade, this time it was no slow seduction, but a hot, maddening conquering that left her reeling. She'd never thought kisses could be so wicked, so tempting into the world he dangled before her, one of passion and pleasure.

Cecilia wanted so much to have a marriage with such emotion as Lord Aaron brought forth in her, and tonight, if only this night she would take whatever he was willing. She would not enter her future of reduced circumstances without knowing the touch of a man. And not just any man, but Lord Aaron.

A curl of hair tickled her back, and she pulled back, reaching up to fix her coiffure. "We should return to the ball before we're noticed missing."

Hunter rubbed his thumb across her bottom lip. She clasped his hand and kissed the digit.

"I'm mad for you, Lia. Be my–"

The sound of someone clearing their throat sounded a little distance away, and Cecilia wrenched back looking up to see who had caught them, only to see the Duchess of Athelby.

"I've come to fetch Miss Smith. Her father has arrived

to collect her, and Cecilia I should warn you, he's made a spectacle of himself."

Dread pooled in her stomach. "He knows I was attending Sir Colten's ball this evening, why would he arrive like this." She stood, and cast another glance at Hunter who met her gaze, hunger raw and unsated even at the news of her father's arrival. "I best go. I will see you again Lord Aaron. Good night."

He stood and bowed, and taking the duchess' arm, she headed indoors. They didn't go back through the ballroom. Instead, the duchess brought her around to the foyer through a servants door that led out near vegetable gardens.

"While I cannot pretend not to know what you were doing outside with Lord Aaron, as your friend I feel I must caution you, Cecilia."

Cecilia slowed her steps, frowning. "It was only a kiss, your grace. Nothing more." Cecilia knew it to be a lie as soon as she uttered the words. It had not been just a kiss. For her, it had been everything, meant everything. Somewhere along her crazy few weeks with his lordship, she'd fallen in love with the man.

"Lord Aaron is a rake. And as much as I adore him, love him as a friend, I worry that your attachment to him is more than his lordships. I do not wish to see you hurt."

The duchess was too kind to care for her, even if she were the marquess's friend also. Cecilia shook her head. "Please do not worry. I'm more than aware that I have no future with the marquess."

The duchess nodded, continuing toward the foyer. "Your father is not pleased. He's stated that he was not aware that Lord Aaron would be present this evening and that the duke and I are trying to sully your reputation by playing your friends. Not actually being one."

She sighed. Hating that her father could do such a thing to her and the two people in the *ton* she trusted with her whole life, not excluding Lord Aaron of course. "I'm so very sorry, your grace. The man my father wishes me to marry no doubt has been watching Lord Aaron's movements and notified my father. I hope we can still be friends after my father has acted so atrociously."

The duchess took her hand, squeezing it a little. "We shall always be friends, and nothing your father says or does will change that. But I think considering our current location, you should go with him without a word. Words between you two can happen when you're in the privacy of your own home."

Cecilia nodded and walked into the foyer spotted her father pacing the space like a caged lion. "Father." She curtsied, taking her shawl from a waiting footman who held it. "Shall we go?"

He slapped on his hat, and without uttering a word of goodbye to the duchess, followed her from the ball. It wasn't until they were in the carriage that his temper frayed.

"How dare you daughter, go to a ball with a man I have expressed my dislike for. Did you know he's a gambler, a man with a string of mistresses about town? The rumours that came across my desk this evening stated that the reason you've been nursing this man back to health is because he cannot hold his liquor?"

"Who divulged this to you. Mr. White? Not the most reliable source, father."

Her parent squirmed on his seat the little muscle in his jaw flexing. "It is little consequence who told me. The truth of the matter is that it is true. And why were you not with the duchess upon my arrival. Where were you, child? Were you with him? Alone?"

"And so what if I was? I'm sick and tired of men like you telling women what to do. You may threaten me with your money and threaten to hurt my charities, but I no longer need to bend to your rules. I have found another sponsor for my charities, and have secured myself employment, so I shall not have you speak to me in such a way. If I were a boy, you would not be sitting here, lecturing me, you would be slapping me on the back, congratulating me on my folly."

"You sullied yourself with Lord Aaron!" her father flopped back into the squabs, clasping his chest. "Oh, the shame."

Cecilia swallowed, wondering how truthful she should be. She erred on the side of caution. "Of course not. I was simply at a ball where my father arrived and dragged me home like a naughty little child. Not a woman who was simply at a ball."

"There is no need for you to even attend such events and there will be no talk of you leaving home and finding employment. You're marrying Mr. White. The contracts have been drawn up, both the marriage contract and that of the contract regarding the inheriting of my firm. The banns will be called and in one month you shall be Mrs White."

"Are you listening to me, father. I said I will not marry Mr. White. Ever."

Her father leaned forward, pointing a finger at her face. "You've said that for years, Lord Aaron and his set is not a life that you would look for. That you loathed the *ton* and their foppish ways, their gossiping and inane lifestyle. Mr. White suits you, and he loves you I'm sure. Given time I'm positive you'll make a happy marriage and give me grandchildren."

The carriage rocked to a halt before their home, and

without waiting for a footman Cecilia jumped down, hurrying into the house. She could hear her father behind her, and even when he called out to her as she made for the stairs, she ignored him. Just as he ignored her, in all that she was and everything that she did.

CHAPTER 11

Hunter lay on the daybed in his library and smoked a cheroot. He watched the flames lick the wood in the grate while his mind fought with the notion of Cecilia being ostracised by her family, becoming a tutor and removing herself even more from his social sphere. It would never do and to imagine her living in such reduced circumstances, well, it wasn't to be borne.

The library door opened and he sighed, closing his eyes. "I'll not be needing you any further tonight, Thomas. You may retire." The patter of footsteps didn't halt, and he sat up, throwing his cheroot into the fire. "Miss Smith," he said, not believing she was standing beside him, here, in his library and alone. Quite alone. "What are you doing here?"

"May I join you?"

A blush bloomed on her cheeks, and he climbed off the daybed, going to her before she could run away. "What are you saying?" Before he touched one inch of her, he wanted to hear exactly what she meant. Not just assume. As a man who had slept with too many women when under the cloudy haze of drink, tonight he wanted to remember every little ounce of detail. Know when the day dawned tomorrow that the memory of her, the smell of jasmine that would touch his bedding, would bring forth all the delicious details of him making Lia *his*.

Cecilia boldly met his gaze. "I'm saying, I want to be with you in every way a man and woman can be together."

A fierce blast of need burned through his veins. He wanted to haul her into his arms so badly. He clenched his hands to his side to stop their shaking. Though he wanted her as his mistress, if he could have this one moment, this beautiful memory of being with her he would take it, and treasure it for this lifetime and the next. With her fierce independence and bluestocking ideals there was no certainty that she would agree to his terms.

Hunter took in her attire, a heavy dark cloak covered her gown, and a bonnet tied tightly beneath her chin helped conceal her identity should anyone have seen her enter his home. He walked to the windows and pulled the drapes closed, then told the footman near the front door to bolt it and go to bed.

Coming back into the library, he shut and locked the door. Cecilia had removed her bonnet and gloves, but the cloak remained. Hunter was fine with that, it would enable him to strip it from her body, like opening a present.

He strode over to her and clasping her face, kissed her soundly. She didn't shy away from the onslaught of his desire for her, if anything she met him, stepped into his hold and kissed him back. Her innocence pulled at him, and he consciously slowed his desire, reigned back his need to take it slow. She was a virgin after all, not used to a man's touch.

"You're so beautiful," he said, pulling the ribbon that held her cloak closed at the neck. Slowly, the tie pulled free, and he slipped the cloak over her shoulders, it hit the floor with a heavy thump.

His breath hitched when he saw what she wore beneath, or better yet, what she hardly wore. A fine, silk chemise did little to hide Lia's figure, thanks in part to the fire that burned behind her, making the material almost translucent. Reaching out, he followed the delicate embroidered pattern across her chest to where he could see her pinkened nipple puckered beneath.

He watched her, as slowly, he traced the circular flesh, loving how it beaded harder beneath his touch.

"You said at Earl Leighton's ball that you were mad for me," she gasped, half moaned.

How he loved that sound and wanted to hear more of the same. "I did," he breathed, leaning down to kiss where he was teasing her flesh, needed to feel that little bud in his mouth, wanting all of her and at once if he could.

"I'm mad for you too," she whispered into his hair. "Please keep doing what you're doing."

Oh, he would and more so before the night was out.

Her breast was heavy, and soon the silk chemise merely became a barrier he was no longer so patient to work with. Standing before her, he slowly untied the ribbons that ran between her breasts, her breathing laboured, her skin flushed with desire.

He'd dreamed of such a vision. Had wanted this for both of them for so long, maybe even from the day she'd saved his life on the street, had pulled him out of the way of the carriage.

There were not many people, least of all a delicate woman who'd put themselves into peril as Miss Smith had. But her generosity of character, her unfailing support and determination to help others was a character he'd come to admire in her and of course saving a drunken fop, as he was, was merely another thing thrown before her that she had to deal with.

Thank the good lord that she had.

The chemise gaped at her front and meeting her gaze he slid the shift from her shoulders, leaving her as bare as the day she was born. His need for her made his body ache and pulling his own shirt from his breeches, he dragged it off and threw it away into the shadowed room.

Not willing to stand idle, she reached out and touched his chest. The feel of her fingers on his body sent heat coiling through his blood, and he took a calming breath to steady himself. He was not a green lad on his first experience with a woman, he'd done this a few times now, but tonight, before this woman, he was like a ship, plummeting at sea.

"I've never felt a man before. You're harder than I imagined you to be."

He nodded, unable to form words as her hand ran down his chest and across his stomach to stop at the front of his breeches. Hunter didn't need to look down to know his member strained against his frontfalls.

And yet she did not halt her inspection of him. Her fingers slid across his breeches before her hand cupped him fully. There was no masking his groan, nor was there any chance that he could deny himself her a minute longer.

He scooped her up, taking her lips in a fierce kiss before throwing her onto the daybed, laughing as she bounced once, her breasts rocking with the action.

Hunter fumbled with his breeches, ripping open his frontfalls, pushing them down and off. He kneeled on the bed and crawled up her body so as not to frighten her away with the size of him. The less she saw of him down there the better. He'd not missed the uneasy flare of her eyes that told him of her unease at the decision she made, but he would not hurt her, tonight she would feel passion, ecstasy and care. Nothing else.

Her fingers slid over his shoulders and pulled him down for a kiss. Willingly he went, the taste of her on his lips an elixir he'd never tire of. The hint of jasmine came from her hair, and her skin shone in the firelight like a beacon of what he could have, of what he wanted for himself from tonight and this day forward.

He kissed her with all that he felt for her but couldn't voice into words. Reaching down he pulled her leg to sit up on his hip and the hair on her mons pressed against his engorged cock. Unable to deny himself, he rubbed against her heated flesh and could've died with the pleasure of it when she pushed up against him, instinctively and wantonly seeking her own release.

"Please, Hunter. I cannot—"

He could no more deny her as he could deny himself, and taking himself in hand, guided his cock against her wet, hot core.

Damn, she was tight as he pushed slowly within her. Lia bit her lip and watched him, only the slightest flicker of pain passed her visage as he breached her maidenhead. He pulled out before guiding himself in again, relief pouring through him when he had no resistance, only sweet acceptance. Delight pierced him when she wrapped her other leg about his hips, holding him firmly against her body.

"This is so wonderful," she mewled, arching her back as he took her.

Hunter forced himself not to release before she'd found hers. He wasn't a selfish lover, ever and he wasn't about to start now.

Their joining became frantic and clasping one ass cheek he ground himself hard against her, relentlessly taking her. He shouldn't, of course, treat her in such a way, a maiden, a woman with no prior idea of what was before her, and yet she did not balk at his lovemaking. Did not ask him to stop, if anything the sounds that came from her urged him on, begged him to do more of the same.

And so he did.

"Hunter," she gasped her fingers pressing hard against his shoulders. "Don't stop, don't stop."

"Never." He thrust once, twice and she shattered in his arms, her sex clamping his own and with a cry, he found his release. He didn't stop until they were both spent, every last ounce of pleasure pulled from their loins.

Hunter flopped beside her, pulling her into the crook of his arm. Both their breathing laboured and he smiled, unable to wipe the grin off his face.

"Was it what you imagined?"

He felt her smile against his chest as she kissed him there before running her hand up to cup his face. "It was more than I could ever imagine."

⚜

THE FOLLOWING afternoon Cecilia took a sip of tea in her mother's parlor and tried and failed to censure her tone towards Mr. White. "I'm sorry, but can you repeat what you just said?"

He sat on the chaise beside her, his eyes bright with expectation. "I said, Miss Smith, that today the first of four banns will be called, marking our betrothal as official. The documents are now all in order, and your father has confirmed that you're to be my wife and so now you may show your gratitude."

Cecilia clenched her teeth. "My gratitude? I will admit to believing you capable of anything, especially after mauling me in the carriage, but to hear that my father has gone through with securing my hand to your own, after all that I told him is not going to bring forth gratitude from me, sir. It'll bring pain and misery. I will not marry you."

His expression hardened. "It is done, my dear. If you cry off, you'll look like a flirt, a woman of loose morals and character. The shame on your father will be too much for him to bear and may injure his constitution."

As much as she loved her parents, had hoped they had the best only in mind when it came to her, this decision of theirs proved they did not. "I'm not a virgin, Mr. White. I have slept with another man and may be right now carrying his child."

If she had hoped he would stand, bow and make a hasty exit she was mistaken.

"Being of the age that you are, and that we are not high Society, I had wondered if you would remain chaste until your marriage, if you ever married that is. But if you told me such things with the mind that I would break the contracts, then you are greatly mistaken. With you comes your father's law firm. Years of clients, families and money that I have worked so hard to keep, only to lose it at the last hurdle. You, my dear, are that hurdle, and I care not that you are chaste. It will merely mean you may be free with my body prior to the wedding. We do not have to wait until the wedding night."

Horror ran down her spine, and she shuddered. "I will never sleep with you, Mr. White. How dare you say such a thing to me?"

His lips twisted in a mockery of a smile. "You're no lady, your actions have shown that this is so, and so what does it matter if you're fast with me too. You'll soon be my wife."

"I'll never be your wife." Cecilia stood and walked away, the thump of her heart loud in her ears.

He followed, clasped her arms in such a tight grip that tears bristled. "Let me go."

"While our conversation today has been most enlightening, I came here to tell you, on your father's behalf that you're to attend the Opera with me tonight. There is a new client your father wants to gain favour with, and so you'll attend as my betrothed. Which of course, you are."

Cecilia wrenched herself free and walked over to the fire, rubbing her arms. "Father has not mentioned this to me before."

"The family have only just arrived in town from their country estate, and he's managed to gain a box beside theirs. And so," he said, leaning down on the chair and picking up his black gloves. "You will do the pretty, smile and be most congenial. You shall pretend to be happy and happy with me, or I shall notify your father of your disobedience. I very much doubt he'd appreciate hearing his daughter has whored herself out."

"You black-hearted blaggard. Get out." Cecilia raised her chin a chill slicing through her veins.

He stormed over to her, clasping her chin in a punishing grip. "Do as you're told Miss Smith, or you'll find when we're husband and wife, the money for your charities will also stop. Be an obliging, faithful and dutiful wife and all will stay well."

Cecilia clasped the mantle for support when the door closed behind him. She would attend tonight, for her father's sake, but then this would be the last time she would be obliging. The funding for her charities was secured as was her own employment. She did not need Mr. White, her father or even Lord Aaron to rescue her. After tonight, Cecilia would commence the future that she'd chosen and revel in her decision. No man would threaten her into a life of misery. Not now or ever.

CHAPTER 12

The Opera at Theatre Royal, Covent Garden, was full to the brim with Society out to enjoy the famous Sarah Siddons who was in town to play Lady Macbeth. Their box did, in fact, sit alongside the esteemed and wealthy family new to town and recently returned from abroad due to the elder Mr. Grant passing away and the massive inheritance now bestowed on his namesake.

Mr. White's entire conversation was directed to the Grants. In fact, he'd spoken of little else. And the more Cecilia learned about the man her father had betrothed her to, the more she realised the man was a scheming, heartless rogue looking for nothing but how to fill his pockets with coin.

"I think my discussion with Mr. Grant went well, what do you think Cecilia?" Mr. White asked, casting another glance in the direction of Mr. Grant's box and receiving a nod in return from the gentleman.

"Yes, it went very well. Father will be happy." Cecilia kept her smile pasted on her mouth, and yet it took every effort to keep it from falling. She wanted nothing more than to leave.

Mr. White droned on, and she kept her eye on the stage as the main attraction for this evening's opera stepped onto the stage to a round of applause. It wasn't until Mr. White's hand slid atop her own in her lap that she was pulled from her own musings.

With her smile firmly in place, she said, "Remove your hand, Sir. I neither seek nor like you touching me in this way."

Anger lit in his eyes briefly, then his expression smoothed to icy civility. "We are engaged, there is nothing wrong with me holding my betrothed's hand."

She pulled free, chuckling as if he'd said something funny when Mr. Grant in the box beside them caught her action. Thinking of her father's firm, she hooked their arms instead, leaning into him as if to whisper a secret. "If you keep being familiar with me, Mr. White I shall walk from the box, whether the gentleman you wish to do business with sees my escape or not. Is that understood?"

Mr. White glared, but sat up, returning his attention to the opera singer. "You have no power in this, Cecilia. Do not threaten me or I shall marry another, and you'll never inherit your father's precious business."

Cecilia listened to the beautiful Sarah play out her role and ignored Mr. White for the remainder of the first half. She glanced about the theatre, but couldn't see anyone she knew. Footmen came about the stalls and started to light the sconces and notified everyone supper and drinks were served in the foyer.

They made their way downstairs, Mr. White taking the opportunity to continue to hold her hand firmly atop his arm. "You do not have to walk so close to me, sir."

"I wish for all to see that we are happy and betrothed. What is wrong with that?"

"Nothing would be wrong with such a thing, had the woman involved not been forced into the situation. A situation that is not of her choosing or liking."

"Miss Smith, good evening."

Cecilia jerked and turned to see the Duke and Duchess of Athelby smiling before her, although their gazes were a little guarded. She curtsied. "May I present Mr. White? He is a solicitor at my father's practice. Mr. White may I present the Duke and Duchess of Athelby."

He bowed. "Your graces, a pleasure to meet you." Mr. White caught the location of Mr. Grant. "If you'll excuse me, there is someone that I need to speak to."

Cecilia bit her lip, not at all liking the duchess' frown. Was she upset with her? Had something happened to Hunter that she wasn't aware?

"Cecilia, what is going on?" the duchess whispered, leaning toward her to ensure privacy.

"A question that we're all in want of being answered."

She gasped, turned to see Lord Aaron towering over her. The pain she read in his gaze tore at her soul, and Cecilia wanted nothing more than to reach out and assure him all was well. That her being here tonight meant nothing to her, only her parent.

"I read the oddest thing in the paper this morning. It was about an upcoming marriage of a Miss Cecilia Smith to a Mr. White. I read it twice in fact, maybe even more than that for I thought it must be wrong. Was I wrong?" he asked, flicking a glance at Mr. White.

The duke and duchess moved away without a word, and Cecilia pulled Lord Aaron to the side of the room, a little distance from the other guests. It afforded them some privacy, but not a lot.

"You did read that right, but–"

"That is all I needed to know." His lordship went to move off, and she clasped his arm, pulling forth some interested stares from those about them.

"Let me explain. Please."

"You're betrothed, and to be married in four weeks. What is there left to know that isn't written in black and white."

"I do not love him, Hunter."

"So you would throw yourself at him without affection." He stood back, his face stoic and hard, but his eyes, they were pools of hurt and she'd put that pain there. At least, her father and Mr. White had, and she'd been too cowardly to do anything about it. Until now.

"My father wanted me to attend here tonight with Mr. White because of a potential client."

"That does not explain the fact that you're to be married." He rubbed a hand over his jaw. "I thought that we may have a future. It seems I read you wrong entirely."

"You did?" she asked, a slither of hope arrowing through her. "You never stated such a thing before."

He glanced about the room, breaking eye contact with her. "I had hoped to set you up as my mistress. To be with me always, where we could be together whenever we wished. I wanted you to be able to have the independence you craved without being beholden to me by law."

Heat bloomed across her face, and Cecilia took a calming breath as the room spun. *Mistress*. The hope she had for them crumbled at her feet and no matter how she tried, she could not stem the tears that fell unheeded down her cheeks.

Hunter reached out, before checking himself and clasping his hands behind his back. "Please, do not cry. I cannot comfort you here."

"No, I suppose you cannot. You only wish to comfort me in the home you'd no doubt set up for me. A little place where you could use me as your whore, whenever the urge struck."

His eyes flared before his mouth tightened into a thin line. "It would not be like that."

"Really? Being your mistress wouldn't be like being your mistress. I'm sorry Lord Aaron, but I'll never be your personal whore."

"What do you want? Marriage?" he asked, frowning.

Cecilia shook her head, not comprehending where this conversation had gone. "Of course marriage. I thought you were different from the peers around us. I thought you cared for me to see past my breeding. It seems I've been a fool."

He checked the whereabouts of other guests, but everyone seemed occupied with their supper and conversations. "I'm the Marquess of Aaron. I'm expected to marry a woman of rank and property. But that does not mean we cannot be together. I do not wish to lose you, Lia."

"Don't ever call me that again," she said, glaring at him. "Your actions tonight are not that of a gentleman, nor are you worthy of me or my love. I reject your offer, my lord. Find someone else to lie on their back for you."

His eyes searched hers a moment before he bowed and walked from the room. Cecilia watched as the duke and duchess followed his lordship. Disappointment swamped her, and she took a fortifying breath. She would not crumble here, show the *ton* that the man she loved had killed all that she'd hoped and dreamed for when she had been wrapped in his arms. Deep inside she'd known their position in Society would make a marriage unlikely, but how she had hoped, especially after the sweet, yet fiercely passionate way he'd made love with her. Swallowing back the tears of pain and piercing disappointment, she hurried away, not wanting anyone here to see her hurt.

Stumbling outside, Cecilia hailed a hackney cab, wanting to return home as soon as she could. Giving the driver the direction, she jumped up into the equipage, hugging herself to stem off the flood of tears that burned her eyes. What a fool she'd been. A silly, naïve nincompoop.

She should've known his lordship would never look to her as his wife and she'd been silly to have ever entertained the idea. Tears slid over her cheeks and she gasped, trying to calm herself. All to no avail, as the hurt won out and she sobbed, quite uncontrollably all the way home, and most of the remainder of the night.

CHAPTER 13

The following week Hunter sat in his library at Yardley Hall, his country estate and battled with his will. Will to do as he should, and will to do what he wanted, craved, longed for.

His mouth salivated at the amber liquid that sat in a crystal tumbler before him. The decanter full to the brim and the scent, strong and cutting called, beckoned him to taste. Just once, a little sip. It wouldn't hurt. He would only have one.

Hunter licked his lips, reaching for the cup before throwing himself back in his chair, rubbing a hand over his face. The last week he'd run a kaleidoscope of emotions. Those of anger, hurt, resentment. Right now he'd do anything to apologise to her, tell her he was sorry for insulting her in such a way. Never did he ever wish to hurt her.

He stood, paced before the decanter of whisky, willing it to be in his mouth. How he wanted to feel the burn as it slid down his throat, to throw him into oblivion where he'd not have to think about Lia and what his proposition meant. That she now hated him. Knew him to be the cad the *ton* knew him as. A man who practically stated she was not worthy of him, not good enough. He sat and picked up the glass, breathing in deep the woody scent.

The drink held the temptation of numbness, a place where he'd no longer hurt. For the pain of losing Cecilia was enough to rip him in two. With a bellowing shout, he threw the glass into the fire, shattering it into a million pieces before swiping the decanter off the table and removing the temptation to fall back into that pit of hell.

He'd fought hard to step away from losing himself in that way, and the loss of Cecilia, while it hurt now, and would hurt for many months to come, their hard work to get him well would not be in vain.

He would not fail in that as well, nor would he allow her to think she was only good enough to be his mistress. The last week had been torture, he'd missed her, dreadfully so and would not allow his error, his rank to determine whom he wanted to be his wife.

There was only one real choice as to who that should be. Hunter stood, starting for the door. No time like the present in winning back the woman he loved and would only ever love.

❦

CECILIA SAT on her bed in the small room at the Spital-fields orphanage and thumbed through papers regarding the charity's latest pupil who'd only arrived yesterday after being dropped off by her mother, a very sickly woman who stated she could no longer look after her four year old child.

Cecilia had ensured she'd been placed near her room and with some of the older girls who promised to take care of her when she wasn't about. The past week had been horrible, her mind muddled and hurt over Lord Aaron's proposal to her.

Not that she would ever consider being his mistress, but the fact that all the time she had been falling in love with his lordship, he'd been merely thinking of a way to make her his mistress. Never had she been so mortified, not even now when all of London found out she'd called off the understanding with Mr. White or that she was now living in reduced circumstances. None of that seemed important when the man one loved found you wanting and unworthy.

A light knock sounded on the door and placing her papers on the small wooden desk that sat before a window, a chair, fireplace and bed the only furnishings the room beheld. It was a small space, but it suited her well enough.

"Come in," she said, picking up her shawl and placing it about her shoulders as her visitor stood within the threshold.

"May I really come in?" Lord Aaron asked, working the gloves in his hand, so they twisted back and forth.

Her body tingled at the sound of his voice. How she'd longed to hear it again, foolish as that thought was. "No, you may leave." Cecilia sat at her desk, fussing with her papers. She had nothing to say to him, nothing she wished to import. His lordship had made his opinions and stance very clear last week, and they did not need to repeat the conversation.

She heard him step into the room, the door closing behind him. "I'm sorry, Cecilia."

Cecilia stared out the window, the anger and pain that she'd been pushing down deep into her soul erupting like a volcano. "You're sorry? I think not. Had you ever cared for me at all, even in the slightest way, you could never have asked me to be your mistress. I may not have your rank, but I have a family, my reputation. How could you ask such a thing from me?"

He took the three steps that separated them and kneeled at her feet, clasping her hands. His piercing blue gaze earnest. "Because I'm a fool who didn't know that the feelings I had for you were not merely lust, but so much more than that. This past week, knowing that I hurt you, insulted you in such a way has broken me. I don't pretend to be a perfect man, by God you know more than anyone that I'm not, but I kneel before you, this very day saying that I do not wish for you to be my mistress, but my wife. Nothing less will do."

Cecilia blinked away her tears and fought to control her emotions. "I'm penniless and as you can see, a woman who no longer has a family. How would the marquess stomach such a woman as your wife? You'll come to regret your choice, and I do not want such a marriage. I will not be anyone's disappointment."

He shook his head, clasping her hands tighter. "I cannot prove to you today that what I say is the absolute truth, that I shall love, care and worship the ground you walk on for the rest of our lives. All I ask is you allow me to prove it in time. I promise I shall not fail you again. I shall never insult your person ever again. You saved me from myself, and for that alone, I owe you my life, but that is not the only reason I love you. Your compassion, care, unfailing determination to make others' lives better shames me. I've been the most selfish being all my life, a family trait I think and one I no longer wish to be. I cannot live without you, and I do not wish to. Please accept my proposal and marry me. You are the love of my life, Miss Smith. My one and only love."

Cecilia sniffed her body shaking with happiness. Could this be true? Did he really mean all that he said?

Hunter reached into his pocket and pulled out a piece of parchment, handing it to her. "What is this," she asked, opening it slowly.

"Read it." He smiled, waiting.

Cecilia quickly scanned the document, refolding it once she'd read it entirely. "Are you trying to buy my love, my lord?"

"I will do anything, will try anything to hear you say yes to my proposal."

"I thought you said you'd never give me the building on Pilgrim Street."

Hunter stood, and picking her up and depositing her on his lap. "It seems I was wrong. Consider it an early wedding gift, if I may be so bold."

She couldn't hide the grin that tweaked her lips. "I'm open to these types of gifts. And I'm in mind to accept your proposal. If you truly mean it."

"Yes, I mean it more than anything."

She clasped his cheek, catching his gaze. "Then yes, so do I."

❧

HUNTER KISSED HER GENTLY, wanting to linger, but there was more to be said. "I shall purchase and remodel any and all the buildings you want. I shall throw all the money I have, which is more than we'll ever spend on the children you so love if only you'll forgive me for hurting you so."

She kissed him back, and for a moment Hunter lost all thought as she wrapped her arms about his neck, kissing him with as much passion as he'd ever felt.

The touch of her hands against his chest, clasping his shoulders, the little mewling gasps and moans shot heat to his core, and his cock hardened. He'd denied himself everything the last week, drink, food, personal grooming, but right now none of that mattered, he would feed off her.

Clasping under her legs, he lifted her and sat her on the small desk, never breaking their kiss. Her gown was heavy and made for manual labour, and reaching down, he slid the garment slowly up her leg, taking the opportunity to feel her stockinged soft flesh on her legs.

"Here, Lord Aaron? Is that wise?" she asked, grinning up at him, her eyes sparkling with mischief.

"No, but we're going to in any case." He fumbled with his breeches, just freeing himself enough to have her. He needed to be with her again, to know that she was his and he was hers.

The soft, tentative touch of Lia's made him groan, and as much as he wanted to claim her, he allowed her to stroke him, feel and learn his body. Damn, it felt good. Too damn good and when her thumb wiped over the top of his cock he groaned.

"I need you, my love," he whispered, aching for her.

She shuffled closer to him on the desk, guiding him within her all the while keeping her eyes locked on his. To see her close the window to her soul at the pleasure of their joining ignited a fire Hunter doubted would ever be doused.

He wanted nothing but to make the woman in his arms happy, loved and cherished and from tonight onwards that's exactly what he would do.

❦

CECILIA WRAPPED her legs about Hunter's back and held him close. She clutched to him as he took her, a feral edge to their lovemaking. His hands gripped her hips and bottom hard, holding her in place, relentlessly taking her hard and fast on the desk. It was the most exhilarating, and naughty thing she'd ever done in her life.

And she loved it.

Her whole centre zeroed in on the place of their joining, the growing pleasure, the tension that increased with every stroke, every gasped breath against her ear, each wet and desperate kiss.

"Hunter," she moaned, clasping his face to kiss him. "I'm-"

"So am I," he gasped.

His strokes became frantic, deeper before unable to deny herself the release she craved, the tension coiled to a point of no return and she tumbled into waves of pleasure, endless delectable loveliness that she'd never tire of.

Hunter groaned her name, sending shivers down her spine as he too found his release, seizing her tight against him as they both regained their breaths.

"I know it has been seven days, but those seven days were the worst of my life. I thought I'd lost you by my own stupidity, my own pretentiousness."

Cecilia laughed, kissing him. "I am not blameless in this. I judged your Society without really knowing them. I too have faults that I shall work on redeeming."

He tilted her chin up to catch her gaze. "I'm going to spoil you and all the children who enter your charities, and God willing our own. I love you," he said, wiping away her tears that would not stop, no matter how wonderful his words. She was a veritable watering pot.

"And I love you, Hunter Always." And forever...

EPILOGUE

Six months later...

C ecilia sat on the floor in a circle of children at the
new orphanage and school on Pilgrim Street. With
Hunter having gifted her the building that had thrown
them together all those months ago, and her purchase of
the second one before their marriage, the buildings had
been joined, renovated and now was one of the cleanest,
structured learning and loving environments that these
children had ever known.

Today she was teaching the youngest in their school
geography and what wonderful natural things in the world
one could see and explore. The bell rang, and all the children looked at her expectantly as it was time for their mid-
morning break. "Remember to clean your hands before
you eat and play safely and fairly. I shall see you
tomorrow."

They waved her goodbye and Cecilia made her way
down to the foyer where she was to meet Hunter. They
were going out for lunch today, but he wouldn't tell her

where the vexing rogue. Not that she minded, she'd allow him anything, especially after all that he'd given her, lavished her charity with money and anything and everything to make the school and orphanage functional.

The bell on the door chimed and in walked her husband. They had been married for six months now, and even after all this time, her parents refused to meet with her. It was the only shadow on their love, but Hunter had been caring and understanding of her pain, and so that made up for a lot of the hurt she hid from the world.

"Coming darling?" he held out his hand, helping her toward the carriage.

"Have I told you today how much I love you?"

He chuckled, holding her hand as she stepped up the carriage steps. "You may love me more after the surprise I have in store for you."

Excitement bubbled up within her, and she could hardly sit still as they made their way through the London streets before stopping at the front of Gunther's Ice Cream parlor. "Is this where you're taking me?"

"This is the first stop, I have another for you, but that journey will take some hours."

He was mysterious and wonderful and the past six months had been the happiest of her life. Exiting the carriage, she took his arm, and they walked into the store. Other women sat about the store eating ices with their friends, and most cast warm smiles of welcome their way, but Cecilia's gaze was locked on who sat at a table near the back of the shop on his own.

They came to stand before the couple, and they stood, a small smile playing about her mother's lips. "Daughter, you look lovely today."

A rush of emotion swamped her, a common occurrence the doctor had said would happen to women in her condition, not because both her parents were here. Parents she'd thought lost forever.

"What are you doing here, mama, papa? I didn't think you wished to see me any longer." They'd been so terribly hurt and angry after she'd married Hunter, marquess or not, the scandal that broke across London that she'd had the banns read regarding one man, and then turned about and married another did cause some salacious talk and no doubt hurt her father's firm, but she would not apologize for the trouble. For that would mean she regretted Hunter and marrying him, which she did not nor ever would.

"We were wrong, Cecilia dear and with your husband's support, he promised us a fair hearing with you to try and make amends. We're sorry for hurting you so, my dear. I truly do not think we were thinking right, nor clear in the least. We wronged you, and I cannot tell you how happy I am that you followed your heart, remained strong under a great deal of pressure that we had no right to bestow on you in the first place. We love you, and want you back in our lives if you'll have us."

Cecilia walked into her father's embrace and hugged him fiercely, swiping at the tears that fell unheeded. "Of course I forgive you both. All I wish from this day on is to forget about our past troubles and start afresh. What say you?"

"We say yes," her father said, kissing her on the cheek and helping her to sit.

"I suppose now is a good time to tell your parents our news, Lia," Hunter said, ordering ices for the four of them.

"What news is this?" her mother asked.

Lia smiled at Hunter, before turning to her parents. "I'm going to have a baby. You're going to be grandparents."

Her father laughed, shaking Hunter's hand and leaning

over to kiss Lia again on the cheek. Her mother wiped at tears and clasped her hand across the small table. "I am very happy for you both. You will be the best mother in the world. With your kind nature and nurturing ways the child will want for nothing," her father said, smiling.

"I do hope so," Lia said, dipping into her ices with a spoon. "But I believe we shall be."

Their outing soon came to an end, and her parents departed, but not willing to leave, Hunter ordered tea for them instead. "I was going to wait until tomorrow when we travelled to my other surprise, but I find I wish to tell you now."

"Really?" she said, taking his hand. "Tell me. What is it, I cannot wait."

"I was listening to your conversation the other week with the duchess and the trouble that's been taking place in Bath and the surrounding district with children and inadequate facilities to deal with the issues that face that town. And so tomorrow you shall inspect a large warehouse that we can convert to help amend this shortfall."

"In Bath?" Cecilia asked, unsure if it were possible to be as happy as she was right at this moment. She'd thought her wedding day had been the best day of her life, but Hunter with his gifts to those in need over the last few months, he kept surprising her, helping her that she was no longer sure what her favourite gift was. "You are too good, darling. I do not deserve you."

"You do deserve me, never say that. I love you, and I adore how you helped me and so many more who have not had the privilege of such an upbringing that we both had by pure chance. I was such a selfish fop for so many years, turned my back not only on myself but the suffering around me. I will not be that person any longer. I do not want that to be my legacy. You inspire me every day, and it is I who hopes to deserve you."

Cecilia moved and sat on Hunter's lap, ignoring the gasped shocks that sounded about them. "You do deserve me, never doubt that my love," she said, kissing him. "Shall we go home, my lord. I wish to be alone with you."

"It seems that I have corrupted my beautiful, honorable wife as well. Whatever shall I do with you."

Cecilia leaned down against his ear and whispered, "Whatever you like."

Dear Reader

Thank you for taking the time to read *To Madden a Marquess*! I hope you enjoyed the second book in my Lords of London series.

I'm forever grateful to my readers, so if you're able, I would appreciate an honest review of *To Madden a Marquess*. As they say, feed an author, leave a review! You can contact me at tamaragillauthor@gmail.com or sign up to my newsletter to keep up with my writing news.

If you'd like to learn about book three in my Lords of London series, *To Tempt an Earl*, please read on. I have included chapter one for your reading pleasure.

Tamara Gill

TO TEMPT AN EARL

Lords of London, Book 3

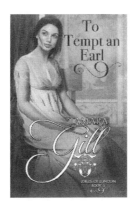

Hamish Doherty, Earl Leighton is having a terrible Season. A portion of his home burned to the ground, he was attacked outside a gaming hell, and a debutante he cannot stomach is determined they'll wed. It's enough to make any lord head for the hills, but his luck turns worse in the country. A large unpaid bill at an inn and a missing purse later, he's ready to concede defeat to the fickle Fates — until rescue unexpectedly comes from an intoxicatingly beautiful stranger.

. . .

As the daughter of a successful tradesman, Miss Katherine Martin has no time for peers and their problems. However there is something about this handsome and yet unlucky earl, and when their paths cross again, Lord Leighton offers to repay his debt to her in any way she pleases. Katherine decides one night in his arms will be just right, and yet as two kindred souls find passion together, it seems one night won't be enough. But can a woman of no rank and trade in her blood be enough to Tempt an Earl?

CHAPTER 1

I t was, without question, the worst week of Lord Hamish Doherty, Earl Leighton's life. He lay sprawled on the main floor of the Two Toads Inn, near the Berkshire border. His eyes watered as pain ricocheted through his face, blood pouring from his nose, that no amount of dabbing with his handkerchief would halt. So much for his unblemished profile, the ladies of the *ton* would be most upset to see that his nose was now a little crooked.

"I told ye, no matter who ye think ye are, if ye can't pay ye debt, I'll belt the money out of ye," the proprietor growled, his bulky frame distinctly menacing.

Hamish swiped at his nose, searching his pockets again for his purse, which was regretfully missing. Where the hell was it? He had it when he arrived three days past, had tipped the busty barmaid a gold coin after a very thorough servicing of his room, but after that his memory was hazy.

He'd gone for a ride yesterday to visit his good friend the Duke of Athelby at Ruxdon house, but with no need of funds there, he'd left his purse in the room. A stupid error of judgement considering the state his nose was now in.

Pushing away a surge of anger, he replied calmly, "This is merely a misunderstanding. I have funds. I left them in my room."

"Are ye saying that they've been stolen? That my inn is an establishment that allows such theft from those who stay under its roof?"

The publican wacked the wooden baton against his hand, a sure sign that would replace the fist that smacked into his nose a moment ago. Hamish looked about the room and cringed that he was now the centre of attention of other guests who were privy to his humiliation. No doubt he'd be the on dit all over town next week once they knew who he was. "Not necessarily...only that I had it when I left yesterday only to find it gone today. And I'm not saying that it was stolen, but only that it's missing, and *I* have not misplaced it."

The barmaid who he'd tupped huffed out an aggrieved breath. "Sounds like ye are trying to pin the stealing on one of us."

Hamish held up his hand when the publican took a step toward him. "I'm not, but I don't have the funds to pay for my debt. Let me send word to my friend, the Duke of Athelby and he'll pay the bill. I assure you." The publican narrowed his eyes and seemed a little less sure of his abuse at the mention of the duke, but it was only short-lived as he seemed to disregard Hamish's lofty contacts and took a threatening step toward him.

"Ye are a liar as well as a lout who cannot pay," the publican accused.

Damn, if there was anything Hamish disliked it was conflict, and he didn't wish to cause trouble so close to the Duke of Athelby's estate, but nor would he allow being treated so poorly. He was a peer, being beaten like a low life criminal. If the publican did not watch his future actions, he would find himself before the local magistrate for battery and theft.

"I'm the Earl Leighton. Do not confuse me for a lout without money or influence. If you come any closer to me with that bat, you'll find out quick enough just how true my words are."

The publican's eyes widened, and his advance stopped. Clearly the man was rethinking better of splitting Hamish's head open. "How do I know ye not lying about being a toff?"

A pair of sturdy boots came up to stand beside his head and he noticed they were well worn and a little dusty, probably from the inn yard. The gown that followed the boots was a dull, grey color, good for traveling. The face that glanced down at him was nothing short of angelic.

"How much does his lordship owe?" this mystery woman asked the publican, stepping between him and the man who'd already given him a bloody nose, which by the way, refused to stop bleeding. He pinched his nose harder.

"Four pounds will cover it, Miss Martin, and may I say how glad we are that ye are here to stay with us again."

She rummaged into her reticule and pulled out the correct amount, placing it into the publican's hand. "Have our luggage moved up to our rooms and have his lordship's carriage packed straight away. As for the gentleman's claims of being Lord Leighton, I can assure you he is who he says. I can vouch for him as we have mutual friends." She glanced at him quickly, her voice no-nonsense and calm. "I'm assuming since he was wanting to pay his account that his intentions were to leave."

"Of course, Miss Martin," the publican said, bowing and yelling out to the surrounding staff to do as she bade. "Apologies, my lord for any confusion. I hope you'll understand not knowing who ye were made me actions necessary."

Hamish glared at the bastard. "Let it be known I shall not shadow your establishment again, and nor will I ever recommend it."

Miss Martin kneeled beside him, holding out her gloved hand for him to take. He did, and she helped him to stand.

For a moment Hamish stared at the angel who'd saved his poor ass without his purse before she raised one, dark eyebrow.

"Lord Leighton, Miss Katherine Martin at your service. We've met before, at a ball I attended with my good friend Miss Cecilia Smith, now the Marchioness of Aaron."

Hamish frowned, racking his brain to place the beauty before him and came up blank. How could he forget such a woman? She appeared a lady who commanded authority and also had a backbone of steel. Even the hefty, large-boned publican didn't seem to faze her.

He met her piercing, intelligent brown orbs that were as dark as a rich coffee and his gut clenched. Upon standing one thing became perfectly clear, she was tall, almost as tall as him. She would never be regarded as a diamond of the first water, but Miss Martin was attractive. Her long, russet brown locks sat about her shoulders, neither tied back or accessorized with a bonnet. She stared at him with unwavering frankness, and as for her mouth, well, sensual and plump were two terms that came to mind...

"I'm embarrassed to say that I do not remember, but I'm very pleased to meet you and I thank you for your help today. I'm unabashedly ashamed of myself. I should have looked after my belongings better."

"I have no doubt that you've been stolen from, and yes, please when staying in such locales in the future, take better heed of your things. I may not always be about to save you." She threw him a grin and turned about on her heel, heading for the stairs.

"Wait!" he said, clasping her arm, gently urging her to face him once again, then releasing her. An inexplicable need to see her again welled inside him. A pretty blush had heated her cheeks possibly because of his familiarity, and he suppressed the urge to pull at his cravat like a schoolboy. "I must repay your kindness. We have mutual friends, shall I see you in town? How can I get in contact with you?" Hamish stopped saying anymore before he sounded like a desperate fool.

She rummaged in her reticule again, pulling out a small card. "We move in quite different social circles, even though my friend has married into the aristocracy. But perhaps we shall see each other again. As for repayment, should you or someone you know ever need a builder, please recommend my father's company. You'll not find more quality or better prices."

Hamish looked down at the card, it read: Mr. Montgomery Martin, Master Builder. "I hope we meet again, Miss Martin." No truer words had he said. She'd saved his hide, stepped in like an Amazonian warrior and fought off the evil publican. The need to meet again, not when he was bleeding like a stuck pig and dishevelled from being assaulted, burned though him. He wanted to see her again within his own sphere, his own terms. He would send a note to the Marchioness of Aaron on his return to London and see what she could arrange.

Miss Martin laughed, heading for the stairs. "Safe travels back to London, my lord. And please, remember my advice for the sake of that pretty nose of yours. I would hate for your bone structure to suffer any more ill effects from a fist."

A warm sensation tugged inside his chest. "So, you think I'm pretty, Miss Martin?"

"I believe I remarked only on your nose, my lord. Is it possible you are fishing for a compliment?"

Hamish chuckled and watched as the impudent, delightful miss walked up the stairs, the last image he had of her the little black boots as they stepped out of sight.

KISS THE WALLFLOWER SERIES
AVAILABLE NOW!

If the roguish Lords of London are not for you and wall-flowers are more your cup of tea, then below is the series for you. My Kiss the Wallflower series are linked through friendship and family in this four-book series. You can grab a copy on Amazon or read free through KindleUnlimited.

LEAGUE OF UNWEDDABLE GENTLEMEN SERIES AVAILABLE NOW!

Fall into my latest series, where the heroines have to fight for what they want, both regarding their life and love. And where the heroes may be unweddable to begin with, that is until they meet the women who'll change their fate. The League of Unweddable Gentlemen series is available now!

LORDS OF LONDON - BOOKS 4-6 BUNDLE

To Marry a Rogue Series
ONLY AN EARL WILL DO
ONLY A DUKE WILL DO
ONLY A VISCOUNT WILL DO

A Time Traveler's Highland Love Series
TO CONQUER A SCOT
TO SAVE A SAVAGE SCOT

Time Travel Romance
DEFIANT SURRENDER
A STOLEN SEASON

Scandalous London Series
A GENTLEMAN'S PROMISE
A CAPTAIN'S ORDER
A MARRIAGE MADE IN MAYFAIR
SCANDALOUS LONDON - BOOKS 1-3 BUNDLE

High Seas & High Stakes Series
HIS LADY SMUGGLER
HER GENTLEMAN PIRATE
HIGH SEAS & HIGH STAKES - BOOKS 1-2 BUNDLE

Daughters Of The Gods Series
BANISHED-GUARDIAN-FALLEN
DAUGHTERS OF THE GODS - BOOKS 1-3 BUNDLE

Stand Alone Books

TO SIN WITH SCANDAL

OUTLAWS

ABOUT THE AUTHOR

Tamara is an Australian author who grew up in an old mining town in country South Australia, where her love of history was founded. So much so, she made her darling husband travel to the UK for their honeymoon, where she dragged him from one historical monument and castle to another.

A mother of three, her two little gentlemen in the making, a future lady (she hopes) and a part-time job keep her busy in the real world, but whenever she gets a moment's peace she loves to write romance novels in an array of genres, including regency, medieval and time travel.

www.tamaragill.com
tamaragillauthor@gmail.com

Printed in Great Britain
by Amazon